PUNISHED WITH LOVE

The moon had risen and everything was enveloped with a light that seemed to come from the gods themselves.

"It is so ... lovely!" Latonia breathed.

"And so are you!" Lord Branscombe replied softly. She felt his arm go around her as he said, "This is where I thought you would want to spend your honeymoon." She felt his lips on her hair before he said, "Long before last night I knew I loved you ..."

"Y ... you ... really ... mean that?"

"Let me convince you." For a moment he looked down at her as if he must impress her beauty on his mind for all time, then his lips were on hers. Then there was nothing else, not even the moon and the stars, but only his arms and his lips ...

Bantam Books by Barbara Cartland
Ask your bookseller for the books you have missed

Barbara Cartland's Library of Love series

Books of Love and Revelation

Other Books by Barbara Cartland

Punished
with
Love

Barbara Cartland

BANTAM BOOKS · TORONTO · NEW YORK · LONDON

PUNISHED WITH LOVE
A Bantam Book / July 1980

ISBN 0–553–13910–X

Published simultaneously in the United States and Canada

Bantam Books are published by Bantam Books, Inc. Its trademark, consisting of the words "Bantam Books" and the por-
trayal of a bantam, is Registered in U.S. Patent and Trademark
Office and in other countries. Marca Registrada. Bantam
Books, Inc., 666 Fifth Avenue, New York, New York 10019.

PRINTED IN THE UNITED STATES OF AMERICA

0 9 8 7 6 5 4 3 2 1

DESIGNED BY MIERRE

Author's Note

There were more than six hundred native States in India in whose territories the British did not directly govern. These were generally those which had accepted the Raj peacefully without fighting. The States varied in size and altogether contained seventy-seven million inhabitants.

Ostensibly they were independent powers, but if their Rulers disregarded the wishes of the Raj, they were given a British Resident or Advisor.

Some of the States were completely independent; others required strict control where the Prince misgoverned his people, oppressed the weak, or had unpleasant habits.

It is amusing to know that Governesses for Princely households were actually supplied by the Raj as a part of the system for Imperial grooming of young Princes. Often this was astonishingly successful!

Moulded by Nannies, Tutors, and Advisors, and by the example of visiting officials and often the schooling of Eton and Oxford, many of the Princes became very English; as someone wrote, "They were English aristocrats buffed to an oriental polish!"

"A sense of greatness keeps a nation great,
And mighty they who mighty can appear."

Chapter One

1883

Riding along the dusty country lane, Latonia wondered why her cousin had sent her such an urgent note early that morning.

It was unlike Toni to sound so agitated, and Latonia found herself going over all the things that might have occurred since they had last been together, which was only the day before yesterday.

It was in fact strange that they had not been in communication for the last forty-eight hours, because, as Toni often said, they were closer than any sisters were ever likely to be.

In fact Latonia often thought that Toni was more like a twin sister, which was not surprising considering that their mothers had felt the same kind of relationship before their daughters were born.

Lady Branscombe and Mrs. Hythe had been first cousins and they had both started their babies in the same month and had laughingly said that they were racing each other as to who would be a mother first.

Mrs. Hythe had won, and Latonia was in fact three days older than her cousin.

To make the unity between them closer, both Lady Branscombe and Mrs. Hythe had been determined to give their children the same name, and, strangely enough, they had been convinced that they would produce daughters.

1

"Hubert naturally wants a son," Lady Branscombe had said. "What Englishman does not? But I am certain, Elizabeth, that I shall have a daughter and that you will have one too."

"That is extraordinary," Mrs. Hythe replied, "because when I have been dreaming about my baby it has always been a girl; and although we have no grand title to inherit, such as makes it imperative for you to have a son, Arthur wants a boy whom he can teach to ride and shoot and who will ultimately go into the same Regiment as he was in himself."

"Arthur will have to wait!" Lady Branscombe said with a smile.

But she did not anticipate, nor did Elizabeth Hythe, that the two girls would both be "only" children.

It was of course obvious from the moment they were born that they would play together and spend as much time as possible in each other's company.

They shared a Governess, which was convenient for the Hythes, who had little money, and it was on Lord Branscombe's horses that Latonia learnt to ride, finding them far more spirited and better-bred than anything her father could afford.

She was, however, not jealous of the difference in financial status between herself and Toni.

Although her father and mother lived in a pleasant but small Manor House with a few acres of ground, she was aware, even when she was very young, that the atmosphere was very different from that in the huge mansion which belonged to Toni's father.

As she had once said to her mother:

"Aunt Margaret and Uncle Hubert never seem to laugh in the way that we do."

But Toni, who had shortened her name from Latonia as soon as she could speak, made up for the lack of gaiety where her father and mother were concerned.

She was not only exceedingly attractive, but she

2

was mischievous, impulsive, and, as she grew older, very flirtatious.

She soon realised that it was not only her social position and her father's great fortune that made her attractive, but her own beguiling and magnetic personality which left young men bemused, bewildered, and head-over-heels in love, almost as soon as they met her.

Lady Branscombe had intended to present Latonia and Toni to the Queen at the same time and give them a London Season, which she was sure would result in both of them finding desirable and eligible husbands.

Unfortunately, Lady Branscombe had been killed in a hunting accident two years before Toni reached her eighteenth birthday, and Lord Branscombe arranged for a distinguished relative to take his wife's place. But Latonia was tragically orphaned a few months before it was planned that she and Toni should go to London.

Captain and Mrs. Hythe had gone to London to visit Lord Branscombe's younger brother.

Kenrick Combe had the reputation of being one of the most outstanding and promising young Officers the Army had ever produced.

He was spoken of with respect by those in command, and with something like awe by his contemporaries.

While he was holding a post of some importance in India, he had asked his brother, Lord Branscombe, to come out and join him, and not only had planned a lot of social entertainment during his visit but had promised to show him those parts of India in which he was particularly interested.

Unfortunately, at the last moment Lord Branscombe found it impossible to leave England.

Not only his duties in the House of Lords kept him, but he was in fact feeling extremely unwell with some complaint which the Doctors were finding difficult to diagnose.

3

They decided that he was not strong enough to undertake such an arduous voyage and the extensive entertaining which was to take place when he reached India.

Therefore, rather than disappoint his brother, he sent Captain Hythe and his wife at the last moment, to represent him.

"It is something Papa will enjoy, as he has always longed to see India," Mrs. Hythe had said to Latonia. "He has also been a friend of Kenrick Combe ever since he was a boy."

"Of course you must go, Mama," Latonia had replied, "but I shall miss you."

"And I shall miss you, darling. But I know you will have fun staying with Toni, and mind you behave yourselves. If there is any mischief about, Toni will be in it."

Mrs. Hythe had laughed at the time and Latonia had laughed with her.

Only when her mother and father had left had she realised how much mischief Toni could manage to pack into twenty-four hours of the day.

She was not yet officially "out" and was therefore supposed to be confined to the School-Room, thinking of her lessons and certainly not of young men.

But where Toni was concerned they sprang up like mushrooms overnight, and there were always notes being surreptitiously delivered to her by servants who had been bribed, assignations in obscure little woods, and riders lurking amongst the fir trees who would appear mysteriously as soon as they were out of sight of the house and ride with them until they returned to it.

To Latonia it was all very exciting and at the same time very innocent.

Sometimes she would ask her cousin:

"Do you think you are in love, Toni?"

"No, of course not!" Toni would reply. "Patrick, Gerald, and Basil are only boys, but I like the look in

4

their eyes when they stare at me, and I enjoy knowing that they are longing to kiss me but are afraid I will be angry if they try."

Latonia laughed, knowing that Toni spoke the truth and was not really interested in any of the men she attracted.

At the same time, she wondered what would happen in the future, and she was also aware that as far as she was concerned, for the first time in their lives she and Toni were very different.

She had no wish to have dozens of men running after her.

In her daydreams she always thought she would find one man whom she would love and who would love her, just as her mother had fallen in love with her father the moment she saw him.

"I want a home," Latonia told herself.

It was something she was to repeat a month later, when, tragically, she learnt of the death of her parents.

She had received a letter from her mother about their trip to India, in which she read:

> *It has all been fascinating, and Papa has enjoyed every moment of it and has so much to tell Uncle Hubert when he returns.*
>
> *I hope you will not mind, dearest, if we decide to stay on for another month. I am sure you are quite happy with Toni, and it will really not be long before we are together again.*

Three weeks before this letter arrived, taking the usual seventeen days to come from India to England, Lord Branscombe died from a disease of the heart.

It was something the Doctors should have diagnosed sooner, and only when it was too late did they realise in what a frail state he had been for a long time and that it was a miracle he had not died sooner.

Telegraphs flashed the news to India, and Toni

realised that her Uncle Kenrick, fifteen years younger than her father, was now the fourth Lord Branscombe.

"What is he like?" Latonia asked.

"I have not seen him for years," Toni replied. "Papa was very proud of him, but from all I have heard he is somewhat of a martinet and the Subalterns serving under him find him terrifying."

She spoke lightly, as though it was of no importance, but Latonia had already heard the servants say that the new Lord Branscombe would be Toni's Guardian.

A month later, on their way back from India, having found it difficult to leave earlier because of the preparations which had been made for their entertainment, Captain and Mrs. Hythe had contracted yellow fever.

A sailor developed it first and this had resulted in the whole ship being quarantined when they reached Port Said.

Mrs. Hythe had written to Latonia saying how frustrating it was to be cooped up in a ship which flew the Yellow Flag and to be prevented from going ashore.

There was, however, nothing they could do about it, and when first one and then another of the members of the crew succumbed to the dreaded disease, and then finally some of the passengers, the Hythes could only pray that they would be immune.

When Latonia learnt that her father and mother had died, it was at first impossible to believe that she would never see them again.

Because she loved her parents and had enjoyed so much happiness with them, she felt as if a part of herself had died with them.

Over and over again she wished that she had been with them so that there would have been no question of their being separated.

Then she told herself that life had to go on, and her father of all people would hate her to be a coward, refusing to face up to the difficulties that lay ahead now that she was alone.

What made it harder than anything else was that Toni had already been taken away to London by a relative who had arranged to chaperone her when she made her début.

"It is no use sitting moping in the country, dear child," she had said. "You must come to London, and although you cannot go to parties because you are in mourning, you can meet people in my house, and as soon as six months are over, you can go to Theatres and the Opera and find a million other things to occupy you."

She had not included Latonia in the invitation, which, as she had only just learnt of her own bereavement, she could not have accepted anyway.

As the months passed and Toni did not return, Latonia realised that the Chaperone had no wish to undertake further responsibilities and that the idea of her "coming out" at the same time as Toni had been conveniently forgotten.

Latonia did not mind. She was quite happy in the country, and an old Governess who had once taught both her and Toni when they were small had moved into the Manor House to live with her as a Chaperone.

Miss Waddesdon was an intelligent woman who was now getting old, and, having no wish for anything but a quiet life, she was content to let Latonia do exactly what she wished.

This, without Toni, amounted to nothing very sensational, and the months drifted past until without any warning Toni returned.

She had no sooner arrived than she sent for Latonia, and as they flung their arms round each other they both knew that nothing was changed and they were back on the same footing as they had been since childhood.

"I have been longing to see you!" Toni cried. "I kept on suggesting to Cousin Alice that you should join me in London, but she was absolutely determined that I was enough trouble on my own."

Toni laughed as she spoke, and Latonia looked at her questioningly as she asked:

"Are you in trouble?"

"Of course I am!" Toni replied. "Am I ever in anything else? And, dearest, you have to help me. I cannot do without you."

"What is it this time?"

"I am in love!"

Latonia clasped her hands together.

"Oh, Toni, how exciting! Who is it?"

"The Marquis of Seaton!"

Latonia gasped.

"I do not believe it! How did you meet him, and what has his father to say about it?"

It was not surprising that Latonia was astonished.

The Marquis of Seaton was the eldest son of the Duke of Hampton, the most important person in the County, who gave himself such airs that he considered the local people beneath his condescension.

Although he could not ignore Lord Branscombe, he had in fact quarrelled with him over the boundaries of their adjoining Estates and the two noblemen had therefore not been on speaking terms.

When they were girls Latonia and Toni had often seen the Marquis out hunting and had longed to make his acquaintance.

He was older than they were, exceedingly handsome, and an excellent rider. But, as Latonia had often thought, it was as easy to meet the man in the moon as to become acquainted with the Marquis of Seaton.

Now it appeared that Toni had not only met him but was in love with him, and Latonia listened with rapt attention to what her cousin had to tell her.

"I saw him almost the first night I was in London," Toni related. "We were at a small musical-party and it was rather dull. I was not surprised when he disappeared before we were introduced, but I was determined to meet him sooner or later. I tried to find out from Cousin Alice who were his friends and which houses he visited."

"Was that difficult?" Latonia asked.

"Not really," Toni answered. "Everyone gossips about everyone else, and I soon discovered that the Marquis was having an *affaire de coeur* with a very attractive married woman."

She thought that Latonia looked shocked, and she added laughingly:

"All men run after married women because they are safe. They never speak to girls if they can help it because they are terrified they might be caught!"

Toni gave a self-satisfied little chuckle as she said:

"It made quite a change for me to be trying to catch one instead of him wanting to catch me!"

"I can understand that," Latonia said. "You look lovely, much more lovely than when you first went to London."

She was speaking the truth.

Her cousin had grown more sophisticated and certainly more alluring than she had been in the past.

Perhaps it was because she was more sure of herself, and of course the gown she wore, which had obviously come from a most expensive and inspired dressmaker, gave her an added glamour.

"Go on about the Marquis," Latonia prompted.

"It took me over a month before I met him," Toni continued, "and when I did, I was determined to make him fall in love with me just to pay him out for all the years that stuck-up Duke never asked us inside Hampton Towers!"

"He would not have asked me anyway," Latonia said.

"You will be asked in the future, because I intend to be the Marchioness of Seaton."

Latonia gave a little gasp.

"What will the Duke say to that?"

"He will have to forget the quarrel he had all

9

those years ago with Papa, and forget his grandiose ideas of marrying his son off to a Princess."

"A Princess?"

"You do not suppose he would think anyone else good enough for the son of an Almighty Duke of Hampton?" Toni answered.

Then she gave a laugh and threw out her arm with an expression of delight.

"Oh, Latonia, Latonia! It has been such fun! I was determined to capture Ivan and I have succeeded, except that in making him fall in love with me, I have fallen in love with him!"

"You really love him?"

"I adore him," Toni replied. "I cannot tell you how attractive and how wonderful he is!"

She gave a little sigh of satisfaction.

"It is like all the fairy stories come true. I love Ivan, he loves me, and everything will be perfect once the Duke has—agreed."

"You are certain he will?" Latonia asked in a low voice.

"He will agree—or he will die," Toni said. "Either way, Ivan and I will be married."

"What do you mean?"

"The Duke is very ill," Toni explained. "I think he has heart trouble rather like Papa had. That is why Ivan has said we must wait a little while before he tells his father that he intends to marry me."

"Supposing the Duke refuses?"

"Ivan is afraid that the shock of his opposing his father might kill him."

"Then you must certainly wait," Latonia said firmly.

"I have told Ivan that I am prepared to do so for a limited amount of time," Toni said. "But he is as impatient as I am for us to be married and be together, so we will not have to wait long."

"You really think the Duke will agree?"

"He will have to," Toni replied, and now there

was a hard note in her voice. "Nothing and nobody will make me give up Ivan, and I know he feels the same where I am concerned. Besides, it is poetic justice!"

"You mean that you will eventually be the Duchess of Hampton?" Latonia asked.

"I mean just that," Toni agreed, "and I shall take great pleasure, Latonia, in inviting all the people to Hampton Towers who have been excluded by that stuck-up, autocratic couple of snobs all these years."

"Toni, you must not speak about your future in-laws like that!"

"Why not?" Toni enquired. "I am not marrying them. I am marrying darling Ivan, and he is a very different sort of person. He is warm and loving and he worships me—he does really, Latonia."

"I am not surprised," Latonia said, thinking she had never before seen her cousin looking so pretty and attractive.

"We are going to be so happy, and I will tell you something that will amuse you: Ivan will find my fortune very useful."

Latonia raised her eye-brows.

"Are you telling me the Duke is not as rich as we thought he was?"

"That is the truth," Toni answered. "Ivan thinks that his father may have mismanaged things and has also over-spent with his grandiose ideas, wishing to appear more important than anybody else. Ivan tells me there are always twelve footmen on duty at Hampton Towers."

"Twelve!" Latonia exclaimed.

"And the Duke travels with six outriders instead of four."

There was silence for a moment, then Latonia asked:

"Has His Grace already picked out the Princess he wishes his son to marry?"

"Of course he has!" Toni replied. "And Ivan says

11

he has the choice of not one but several, mostly from German Principalities but nevertheless of Royal blood."

Latonia was silent.

She was thinking that while the Branscombes were an old and respected family and the new Lord Branscombe was the fourth Baron, they did not compare with the Duke of Hampton, whose ancestors included many members of different European Royal families.

Toni looked at her and laughed.

"I know what you are thinking," she said, "but you need not waste your time worrying about me. Ivan loves me and I love him, and not all the Dukes or a whole barricade of blue-blooded Royal Princesses are going to stop us from marrying each other!"

"Oh, I am glad, dearest!" Latonia said warmly. "Not because you will be a Duchess but because you will be happy as Papa and Mama were. Nothing mattered to them except each other and their love, and that is what I have always prayed both you and I will find one day."

"As I have found already," Toni contradicted. "When you meet Ivan you will understand why he is the only man I have ever met who makes my heart beat quicker and with whom I feel I want to spend the rest of my life."

Riding now towards the Castle, Latonia wondered a little apprehensively if Toni's impetuous summons had anything to do with the Marquis.

'Surely,' she wondered, 'nothing could have gone wrong?'

She had not yet met him, although there was no doubt from the notes that arrived every day, as well as flowers and other presents, that he was as infatuated with Toni as she was with him.

They also managed to meet regularly but secretly, so that their interest in each other was not repeated to the Duke.

As the Hampton and Branscombe Estates marched with each other, there were plenty of woods just on the boundary on each side, where two people on horse-back could disappear amongst the trees, and when they rode home in different directions, no-one would have the slightest idea that they had been together.

"Does not your Head Groom think it rather strange that you ride alone?" Latonia asked.

"It is something I have always done, as you know, except when I am riding with you," Toni answered, "so he is used to it. Once or twice I have told him that I was meeting you."

Latonia gave a little cry.

"Oh, do be careful not to tell lies in which you might be caught out!" she said. "He may know I have no decent horses of my own at the moment."

"Why did you not tell me?" Toni asked. "I will send you over two immediately."

Latonia looked embarrassed.

"I did not mean that."

"Well, you should have. We share everything as we always have, and as soon as possible I want you to move here and be with me."

"I am longing to do that," Latonia answered, "but Miss Waddesdon has been so sweet in coming to live with me after you went to London that I cannot send her away."

"I will tell you what we will do," Toni said. "As soon as that tiresome woman whom Cousin Alice chose is no longer here to chaperone me—and she drives me crazy with her eternal chatter—both you and Miss Waddesdon can come to the Castle."

"That would be lovely!" Latonia said.

"It will make it a lot easier," Toni said with satisfaction, "and with any luck you will be able to move in next week, or the beginning of the week after."

Latonia had been looking forward to it so much

13

because she loved being with Toni, and she thought now it would be very disappointing if Toni's urgent summons meant that their plan had to be changed.

As she rode down the drive and saw the Castle ahead of her, she thought it would be fun to be back in the great house that she had found so intriguing as a child.

There had been so many places in which to play Hide-and-Seek, while the Nurseries, which had seemed as big as the whole Manor House, had held every type of toy, game, and doll that any two small girls could have wished for.

Then as she drew nearer it suddenly struck Latonia for the first time that the Castle in the future would belong not to Toni but to her uncle.

As it was the family house of the Branscombes, Kenrick Combe would live there when he returned from India, and, as Latonia had never met him, she thought perhaps she would no longer be the welcome guest she was now.

Ever since she could remember she had either been staying at the Castle or else running in and out as if she had as much right to be there as Toni herself.

Now almost like a shadow across the sunshine she realised that when Toni married and the new Lord Branscombe was in residence, she would be a stranger, expected to ring the bell and wait for the door to be opened to her.

As if she was determined to enjoy the privilege of being welcome as long as she could, she dismounted at the front door, handed her horse over to a groom, and ran up the steps.

There was only one footman on duty in the Hall and he was busy at the far end of it, tidying some papers that had been blown about in the wind.

"Good-morning, Henry!" Latonia said as she passed him.

He looked round at her and grinned.

"Morning, Miss Latonia."

"Where is Miss Toni?"

14

"Upstairs in 'er room. She said Oi were to send you straight oop to 'er soon as you arrived."

He made no effort to show her the way, since of course it was unnecessary, and Latonia was already halfway up the stairs before he had finished speaking.

She ran along the broad landing at the top of them and hurried towards one of the important bedrooms which Toni had occupied since she had grown up.

Before that Toni, and Latonia when she was with her, had slept on the second floor.

Latonia reached her cousin's door and without knocking opened it and walked in.

Toni, who was sitting staring out the window onto the garden, gave a little cry and sprang to her feet.

"You are here! Oh, Latonia, thank God you are here!"

She ran across the room as she spoke and flung her arms round her cousin. She clung to her as she had done when they were children, when if something was wrong they could find consolation only in each other's arms.

"I came as soon as I received your note," Latonia said. "What has happened?"

"I can hardly bear to tell you," Toni answered.

To Latonia's surprise, her voice sounded hoarse and at the same time frightened.

"You are upset . . . really upset," Latonia said in surprise. "What can have occurred? It is not . . . the Marquis?"

"No, no, of course not," Toni answered quickly.

Latonia felt relief sweep over her.

"I was afraid . . . desperately afraid that something had gone wrong and the Marquis had found he could not . . . marry you after all."

"No, it is nothing like that, and Ivan knows nothing about this."

"Then what is it?" Latonia enquired.

15

There was silence for a moment. Then Toni said in what seemed an almost strangled voice:

"It is—Uncle Kenrick! He is back in—England—and he has—sent for me."

Latonia loosened her arms from round Toni so that she could stare at her.

"I ... I do not ... understand! Why should that ... upset you?"

Toni gave a little sigh.

"I will tell you," she said. "Let us sit in the window-seat."

The two girls moved to the wide window-seat, and with the sun on Toni's face, Latonia could see that her eyes were dark and strangely perturbed.

She put out her hand towards her cousin.

"What is it, dearest? What has upset you?" she asked. "I can see it is something serious."

"That is what I am afraid it may be," Toni replied.

"Tell me," Latonia begged.

Toni sighed again and said:

"It happened about four months ago."

"What happened?"

"A young man I met in London fell in love with me and made rather a nuisance of himself."

"Who was he?"

"His name is Andrew Luddington, and he was home on leave from India."

It struck Latonia as she listened that India was closely connected with Toni's uncle, but she did not speak and Toni went on:

"He was rather good-looking and he danced well, and at first I found him amusing."

"What you are saying," Latonia interrupted, "is that you flirted with him!"

"Of course I did!" Toni said defiantly. "I flirt with everybody, but that does not mean I was in love with him or anything like that."

"N-no ... of course not."

"He became more and more persistent. In fact, as

16

I said, he made a nuisance of himself. Wherever I went he would follow me. He wrote to me three or four times a day, and when I was with him he proposed in a wild and somewhat uncontrolled fashion which, after a time, I found embarrassing."

Latonia did not say anything, but she knew that her cousin had this effect on quite a number of men.

They seemed to lose their self-control where she was concerned, and in the past there had been a number of small incidents, which had shown all too clearly that Toni's attractions made men unbalanced and sometimes unrestrained.

"Go on," she said aloud.

"He grew worse and worse," Toni continued, "until finally I told him I had no wish to see him again."

There was silence, and because Latonia sensed that this was not the end of the story, she asked:

"What did he do?"

"He tried to kill himself!"

Latonia drew in her breath before she asked: "H-how?"

"He used his service revolver, but he failed, perhaps because he was so agitated or perhaps because he was in such a state of emotion that he did not shoot himself actually through the heart, as he had intended; anyway, he survived."

"What did you do?" Latonia asked.

"What could I do?" Toni replied. "I was sorry—very sorry—but it was not really my fault."

Again there was silence until Latonia asked:

"If this happened all those months ago, why does it concern you now?"

"Because Andrew's mother has complained to Uncle Kenrick."

"And he is angry?"

"I imagine—very angry!"

"So he has asked to see you?"

Toni, as if she could restrain herself no longer, burst out:

"He says he is taking me back to India with him! That I have behaved disgracefully and that obviously my Chaperone has no control over me!"

"But you must explain to him ..." Latonia began quickly.

"Do you suppose he would listen?" Toni asked. "No! He is not prepared even to hear my side of the story. I have just received my orders!"

She picked up a letter that was lying on the window-seat and handed it to Latonia.

Before her cousin could read it, she cried out:

"Save me, Latonia! You have to save me! I cannot go to India with Uncle Kenrick at this particular moment! If I do, I shall lose Ivan."

The way she spoke told Latonia what in fact she had suspected, although she had not dared to put it into words even to herself.

The Marquis, far from being completely intent on marrying Toni, was still slightly elusive, still at the stage where, should the marriage upset his father, he would cry off.

There was nothing that Toni had actually said that made her think this.

It was just an impression Latonia had, just a slight tension of which she was conscious, and which, because she knew her cousin so well and they were so much like twins, she had sensed perceptively.

Now she was sure that Toni was speaking the truth when she said that she could not leave the Marquis at this very crucial time in their relationship.

Slowly, because she was trying to think clearly, she smoothed out the pages of the letter, which she thought Toni must have crumpled up in her despair and read them:

My Dear Niece:

I am extremely disturbed by a letter which reached me from Lady Luddington about her son Andrew and also by some other reports that

I have received from friends and acquaintances regarding your behaviour in London.

It appears to me that your Cousin Alice has not chaperoned you as competently or indeed as strictly as your Father would have wished and expected.

I therefore intend, when I return to India in four days' time, to take you back with me, where I think it will be to our mutual advantage to get to know each other better than we do at the moment.

Unfortunately, it is impossible for me to come to the Castle as I had intended, and I must therefore ask you to join me here at the family house in Curzon Street at the very latest by next Thursday.

We shall leave for Tilbury the following morning. I have already booked your passage with mine on the P. & O. Ship Odessa.

I have on your behalf expressed my deepest regrets to Lady Luddington and told her that it is with the utmost relief that I learn that her son is alive and improving in health.

I consider it extremely fortunate that this regrettable affair, which reflects on our family honour, has not become public—nor been reported in the Press.

Kindly let me know at what time you will be arriving at King's Cross Station, and I will send a carriage to meet you.

I remain,
Yours most sincerely,
Branscombe.

P.S. In case it has not been explained to you, I am now, since your father's death, your sole Guardian.

Latonia read through the letter, then raised her eyes.

"Oh, Toni, you have to go, dearest," she said. "As he says, and I thought it as I was arriving here, he is your Guardian."

"I will not go! I refuse!" Toni cried in the defiant manner which Latonia knew of old.

"You have no alternative," she answered. "After all, he controls your money. He can, if he wishes, refuse to allow you any if you disobey him!"

"I hate Uncle Kenrick!" Toni said. "I have always hated what I have heard of him. And I thought secretly that Papa in a way was rather frightened of him."

"How could he be?" Latonia enquired.

"Uncle Kenrick was so clever that he made Papa feel that he was stupid, which no-one else did. And as everybody eulogised about him, it was obvious that Papa felt it unfair that his younger brother should have so much attention."

Latonia remembered that Lord Branscombe had been very conscious of his own consequence, and in a way she could understand that it must have been annoying for him to see so much attention paid to his brother when by right it should have been paid to him.

"When you meet you will be able to charm him," she said consolingly. "You have always had your own way with men, Toni, and I do not expect your uncle will be different from any of the rest."

"Of course he will be different!" Toni replied. "Uncle Kenrick is not a man, he is a relation, and relations are always obnoxious. You know that!"

"With the exception of us," Latonia said with a smile.

"That is different," Toni answered. "You are not a relation, you are part of me just as I am part of you."

She paused for a moment, then said:

"You are lucky. You have no Branscombe relations, only Mama's sweet, charming family, who were all like your mother."

She rose from the window-seat to walk across the room.

"I am not going to India! I am not! I am not! And nothing you can do will make me!"

"I have not said anything yet," Latonia answered, "except that you have to obey your uncle."

"If I go to India I will lose Ivan—I know it in my bones! His father and mother will get at him and tell him how unsuitable I am to be his wife, and because he has always listened to them he will find himself up the aisle with some horrible German Princess before he realises what is happening."

"Surely he is not as weak as that?"

"He is," Toni contradicted, "not that he realises it, but because ever since he was a baby he has been brought up to believe that the only thing that matters is pomp and circumstance, and all that bowing and curtseying."

She made a little gesture with her hands before she went on:

"I have taught him that life can be much more fun. We laugh and enjoy ourselves just because we are people and not puppets to be pulled about on strings."

"And you think when you are not there he will forget how much he loves you?"

"He will still love me," Toni said, "but he will believe it is his duty to do what his father wants, his duty to be a stuck-up, pompous Duke, his duty to spend his time hanging round the Throne."

She spoke so positively that Latonia could almost see it happening.

Then she looked at her cousin's lovely, troubled face and asked:

"What can you do about it?"

"I know exactly what I can do," Toni answered, "or rather, what you can do for me."

She looked across the room at her cousin. Then her voice seemed to ring out as she said:

"You will go to India with Uncle Kenrick!"

21

Chapter Two

Latonia stared at Toni for a moment before she said:

"Of course you are joking."

"No," Toni replied. "I am serious, and you must see that it is the only solution."

"How . . . could I? It is . . . impossible!"

"If you think about it," Toni interrupted, "it is quite simple. Uncle Kenrick has not seen me since I was ten—over eight years ago."

"But he still knows what you look like."

"I look very like you, as you look very like me," Toni replied.

It was in fact true. The two girls were both fair, both had deep blue eyes, and they were the same height.

There was, however, a difference in that while Toni had a mischievous, naughty little face, Latonia's was far more soft and spiritual, and, because she had not the sophisticated polish which London had given Toni, she was far more innocent.

There was something untouched and very young in the expression in her eyes and the softness of her lips, which, unlike her cousin's, had never been kissed.

At the same time, Latonia realised that there was a distinct likeness between them.

"What you are suggesting," she said aloud, "is, of course, impossible. Supposing your uncle discovered the truth? Think how furious he would be."

"He might be angry, but at least if you were in India, or even halfway there, I should be with Ivan; and there is every chance that the old Duke will die within months or even weeks."

Latonia did not say anything, but she had the feeling it was wrong for Toni to wish that anyone should die, even the Duke whom as children they had both disliked because they had never been asked to parties which had been given for the Marquis.

"If you go to India as your uncle wishes," she said after a moment, "I am sure that as soon as Ivan feels that his father is well enough, he will leave him and follow you."

"And supposing he does not do so?" Toni asked in a low voice.

"He loves you."

"I know he does at the moment, but you have no idea how much pressure has always been put on him to remember his position in life, a position that the Duke has blown out of all proportion, into being more Royal than Royal."

Latonia clasped her hands together and asked:

"Are you ... seriously asking me to take your ... place and go to India with your ... uncle instead of ... you?"

"I am not asking you, Latonia, I am begging you on my knees to do so," Toni said. "My whole happiness depends on my staying here with Ivan, on keeping him so much in love with me that however much his father tries on his death-bed to persuade him to marry the Princess, he will refuse."

Latonia could not help thinking it was just the sort of promise the Duke might extort in order to get his own way.

It would be very hard for anyone, especially somebody like the Marquis, who was an only child, to refuse a dying man's wish.

She could understand only too well Toni's apprehension that she might at the last moment lose the man she loved.

At the same time, every instinct in her body shrank from being deceitful in a way that she knew would have horrified her parents.

"I want to help you, Toni," she said, "and you know that I love you, dearest, more than anyone else in the world. But if you persuade me to do anything so outrageous as to pretend to be you, I am afraid I should let you down."

"Why should you?" Toni asked. "We have been so close to each other that we almost think the same, and you know exactly how I would behave in almost any circumstances."

She paused, then with a naughty twinkle in her eye said:

"Actually it will be very good for you. You will have to entice young men into falling madly in love with you, and as you have always been prettier than I, I am sure you will have no difficulty in that!"

Latonia, however, looked at her cousin in horror.

"How could I attempt to do such a thing?" she asked. "Besides, think what your uncle would say! The whole reason for his taking you to India is that he thinks you have behaved badly."

"It is the kind of unpleasant punishment Uncle Kenrick would consider appropriate," Toni remarked scornfully.

"But Mama and Papa were thrilled by India."

Latonia stopped and gave a sudden cry.

"Oh, Toni! They will have talked about me; and supposing, from what they have said, your uncle realises at once that I am not his niece but their daughter, what then?"

"Why should he?" Toni enquired. "As far as I know, you have never been photographed."

"No, of course not," Latonia agreed. "It is far too new and too expensive a novelty to have reached the Manor."

"Then you will be quite safe," Toni said. "If your

24

mother has described you, then she might have been describing me, except that you are 'the good one' and I am 'the bad.'"

"Not bad, dearest," Latonia said loyally, "only slightly unpredictable in what you do and say."

Toni laughed.

"I think Uncle Kenrick will be pleasantly surprised when he meets you, or else he will think I am over-awed by his disapproval."

She put her arms round Latonia and said:

"Oh, dearest, I knew you would save me, and now we have to make plans quickly because, if you are to be in London by Thursday, we have a lot to do."

Latonia still looked doubtful, and Toni explained:

"First of all, the whole household have to believe that I am going to India as my uncle has commanded."

"If they believe you have gone away, where will you stay?" Latonia asked.

"Do not be stupid, dearest; I am going to be you and you are going to be me, so I shall move to the Manor, and the only person who will know about the deception will be old Waddy! You know she would never give me away."

That was true, Latonia thought. When Miss Waddesdon had been their Governess, Toni had always been her favourite, and it was not just because she was employed by Lady Branscombe.

She had always kept any misbehaviour on Toni's part to herself, and if her parents were angry with her she managed to make excuses which mitigated their wrath.

"You really intend to stay at the Manor?" Latonia asked.

"Of course!" Toni answered. "Think how thrilling it will be to meet Ivan there."

"In the ... house?"

"But naturally. I am tired of hiding myself amongst trees that drip on us when it has been raining. He can come into the Manor from the garden and no-one will know he is there except Waddy, who I am quite certain will be only too willing to go to bed early."

"Supposing the Duke finds out?" Latonia asked. "He will be shocked at the idea of your entertaining a man alone without a Chaperone."

"No-one will find out," Toni said confidently, "and it is far safer than meeting him in the woods. The other day we had a very narrow escape when one of the Duke's wood-cutters passed by."

Latonia clasped her hands together.

"Do be careful! You know how people talk. The Duke might forbid the Marquis once and for all to see you again."

"Ivan would not obey his father. At the same time, it would worry him, and because I love him I do not want him worried."

"Of course not, darling," Latonia agreed. "Mama always said that if one loves someone, one wants to protect them from anything harmful or unpleasant."

"That is why you will protect me from Uncle Kenrick," Toni said triumphantly.

Latonia felt she should protest more and, in fact, refuse to do what Toni wished, but because she loved her cousin she knew that she could not risk her losing the Marquis.

She was sure that Toni was right when she said that every possible pressure would be brought on the young man to marry someone whom the Duke would think a suitable wife for his only son.

And that would certainly not be the daughter of his old enemy and neighbour, Lord Branscombe!

'I must think only of Toni's happiness,' Latonia thought to herself, 'and if I can just pretend that I am she, until she and the Marquis are married, then however angry her uncle may be, it will be too late for him to interfere and spoil their happiness.'

At the same time, she knew that she was frightened as she had never been frightened before, not only at acting a part for which she felt she was very badly qualified, but also at going out to India and into a world about which she knew nothing.

Her father and mother had never been able to travel because there had not been enough money, just as there had not been enough money for them to entertain as frequently as they would have liked.

Whatever other reasons they may have had for going to India, it was what her father called a "second honeymoon" and it was in fact the first holiday they had been able to enjoy since their marriage.

As Lord Branscombe was paying all their expenses, it was, as her father had said jokingly, "an added bonus" that they had not sought or expected.

And yet, Latonia thought miserably, if only they had stayed at home they would be alive today.

She felt the tears prick her eyes as she thought of it, then resolutely she forced herself to think only about Toni.

Toni was alone in the world, just as Latonia was, and nothing could be better at this moment than for her to settle down with somebody she loved and have a husband to look after her.

Latonia knew, as no-one else did, that Toni's mischievousness and what was called her "naughtiness" stemmed from the stiffness and lack of love and laughter in her home.

It was impossible for anyone not to feel under restraint when they were at Branscombe Castle, and when Toni had found that the young men of the neighbourhood were attracted to her, it was exciting because they were something new.

"I do not know what Toni would do without you, dearest," Latonia's mother had often said to her. "She may be rich, she may have a very impressive home, but when we leave the Castle I always feel we are leaving behind us a very lonely little girl."

Her mother's words had conjured up for Latonia a picture of Toni standing small and rather unsure of herself in the great Hall with its high ceilings and heavy, dark paintings of Branscombe ancestors.

It was as if a fairy-child had strayed there by mistake and her place was really amongst the flowers in the garden with the wind blowing through the trees in the Park.

Everything that was protective in Latonia now made her long for Toni to be happy, and if that happiness lay with the Marquis, then whatever the sacrifice on her part, she must make it for Toni's sake.

At the same time, it was all a little difficult to sort out in her mind.

"You will be at the Manor, pretending to be me," she said slowly. "But what will happen if anyone should call to see me?"

"Waddy will have to be clever and tell them I am in bed with a cold," Toni replied, "and besides, from all you tell me, you do not receive many visitors."

"That is true," Latonia admitted. "Not since Papa and Mama died."

"There is only one visitor I really want," Toni said with a smile that seemed to illuminate her face. "And it will be lovely to know that Ivan and I can sit in your mother's little Sitting-Room and no-one will disturb us."

"Oh, Toni! Toni, I am sure it is something you should not do!" Latonia exclaimed.

"It is something I have every intention of doing," Toni answered, "and, as I have already said, it will be good for you to see the world, even with Uncle Kenrick glowering at you. And remember, you not only look lovely, but everyone will think you are a great heiress, which to many men is, I assure you, a very good introduction!"

Latonia, however, was not listening to the end of the sentence.

"If I am to look ... lovely," she said hesitatingly, "I shall need to borrow some of your clothes."

"You are going to borrow nearly everything I possess!" Toni replied postively. "Especially all the beautiful new gowns I bought in London."

"How ... can I? What are you going to wear?"

Toni gave her a naughty smile.

"My trousseau!" she said. "I have already planned it. It is going to cost an astronomical amount of money."

"But ... supposing," Latonia said wildly, "your uncle forbids you to marry the Marquis? He can do so, as he is your Guardian."

"It will be too late!" Toni said blithely. "I shall be married, and by the time he comes hurrying back to England I may even be having a baby."

"Toni!"

Latonia's exclamation was one of shocked horror.

Toni laughed.

"Do not be so straitlaced, my dearest. Most people have babies after they are married, and Ivan will certainly want an heir."

"I am sure you should not be ... talking or ... thinking like that," Latonia said.

Toni laughed again.

"I am practical while you have always had your head in the clouds. You still believe that babies are found under gooseberry bushes. It is time you woke up to reality."

The colour rose in Latonia's face, then she said quickly:

"Go on planning how we can enact this absurd, frightening drama so that no-one will be suspicious that we have exchanged places."

"We just have to be clever about it," Toni said. "I shall announce to the household that I have to go to India with Uncle Kenrick. You will help me choose the clothes I shall take with me, and I shall tell you in front of my lady's-maid that I have a lot of gowns for which I have no further use."

Latonia looked as if she did not understand, and Toni said quickly:

"Do not be silly, Latonia. I have to have something to wear when I am staying at the Manor, and I want Ivan to think I look lovely."

"But of course," Latonia agreed. "That is why you must not give me too many things to take away with me."

"Both the servants at the Castle and Uncle Kenrick will expect me to travel with a huge wardrobe of gowns and accessories, and I am quite certain that the people in India will want to see Uncle Kenrick's niece wearing the latest fashions."

"Everything seems to grow more complicated by the minute," Latonia said unhappily.

"Leave everything to me," Toni answered. "All you have to do is to agree to everything I suggest, and no-one will be in the least suspicious that we are not who we appear to be."

"And how do we change over?"

"I have been thinking about that, and I think the best thing would be for me to travel to London by carriage. That will mean you can come with me, ostensibly to see me off, and that tiresome Mrs. Skeffington can be left behind."

Mrs. Skeffington was the Chaperone that Toni's Cousin Alice had sent with her to Branscombe Castle.

She was a middle-aged woman, the widow of an Army Officer who had been killed in Egypt and Latonia could understand all too easily why Toni found her tiresome.

Mrs. Skeffington's only interest in life was to gossip about the people who she thought were socially important, and because she liked the sound of her own voice, she seldom listened to anything anyone else said.

She was delighted with the luxury she found at

Branscombe Castle, and because she hoped to stay on indefinitely in her present position, she toadied to Toni so obviously, so effusively, that it was embarrassing.

"Wait a minute!" Toni said suddenly. "I have an idea!"

"What is it?" Latonia asked.

"You know how much Mrs. Skeffington likes being here? Well, I shall not tell her or anyone else that I am going to India."

Latonia looked at her cousin wide-eyed, and Toni went on:

"This makes everything much safer. I shall just say that Uncle Kenrick wants to see me and therefore I am going to London for a few days to be with him before he leaves. I shall ask Mrs. Skeffington to stay on, and I am sure she will be only too glad to agree. Then when we get to London we shall post my letter to her saying I have left for India and no longer require her services."

"Do you think she will let you travel alone with me?"

"She will let me do anything I want," Toni answered, "and I shall just tell her we are going up together. When we reach London we will not go straight to Curzon Street where Uncle Kenrick will be waiting, but change places somewhere else."

"Where?" Latonia asked.

"We will stop at an Hotel for a few minutes and tell the coachman that that is where Uncle Kenrick is staying and he can go home."

Latonia thought this over, then she said:

"I cannot see why they should be suspicious, but what happens to you?"

"I shall go back to the Manor by Post Chaise," Toni said, "and I will not be frightened of going alone because, as it happens, I have often been in one by myself in order to meet Ivan, without Cousin Alice being aware of it."

31

"I suppose I ought to scold you for that," Latonia said.

"Do not waste your breath!" Toni retorted. "What we have to think about is getting you into a hackney-carriage with all your luggage and going to Curzon Street."

"Surely your uncle will think it very strange, my arriving in such a manner?"

"That is quite easy to explain," Toni said. "Tell him one of the horses cast a shoe as soon as you reached London, and therefore, instead of waiting for a blacksmith, you had the good sense to hire a hackney-carriage so as not to keep him waiting."

Latonia flung up her hands in horror.

"Lies! Lies! Oh, Toni, I shall never be able to make them sound convincing as you do! Your uncle will be suspicious of me from the moment he sees me."

"He will be nothing of the sort!" Toni said. "Stop frightening yourself, Latonia. This is going to be an adventure for you as well as for me. If I were a Fortune-Teller I would predict that somewhere in India you will find a fascinating, charming man with whom you will fall in love as I have fallen in love with Ivan."

"That is extremely unlikely," Latonia answered. "He would think I was you and he would be very disappointed when he found that I was only Cinderella dressed in somebody else's gown to go to the Ball."

Toni laughed.

"If he loved you, that would not matter in the slightest. Although Ivan is delighted that I have so much money, I am sure that he would still love me if I had not a penny. At least I—hope so."

There was, for just a moment, something unsure and a little apprehensive in the last words, which made Latonia put her arms round Toni as she said:

"I am sure that is true, and, dearest, I will do

anything . . . anything you ask of me, as . . . long as it makes you . . . happy."

"I knew you would not fail me, Latonia," Toni said, "and remember, no-one knows what this letter from Uncle Kenrick contains except us."

As she spoke, she picked it up, took it across the room, and locked it away in a drawer of her writing-desk.

"Now," she said, "I shall announce to Mrs. Skeffington and everybody else that it is a terrible bore but I have to go to London to see Uncle Kenrick. I do not know how long he wishes me to stay, but I shall take a lot of clothes rather than have to send back for anything I need."

"I suppose . . . we are doing the . . . right thing?" Latonia asked in a worried voice.

"Anything is right," Toni replied, "as long as I can stay here with Ivan, as long as I do not lose him."

* * *

Three days later, sitting beside Toni as they travelled to London in a huge, comfortable travelling-chariot, Latonia felt more frightened and anxious with every milestone they passed.

She already felt very unlike herself, dressed in one of Toni's new and most expensive gowns with a little velvet jacket which buttoned down the front and, in case the September evening was cold, a small sable tippet round her throat.

Everything she wore was silk, which rustled when she moved, and it was so different from her ordinary clothes that Latonia began to feel she was a creature of someone's imagination.

Then when she saw the enormous number of trunks and hat-boxes that Toni thought were necessary for the journey, she was quite certain that they were all part of a dream from which the awakening would be very unpleasant.

Every night since she had agreed to Toni's scheme, she had lain awake worrying that she was doing the wrong thing, and yet she was not certain what was the right thing.

What would her mother and indeed her father have said at her undertaking such a deception?

At the same time, they too had loved Toni as if she were their own daughter and would certainly have wanted her to be happy.

However, Latonia had at last met the Marquis and was now convinced that he was the right person to be Toni's husband.

When in the past she had seen him in the hunting-field at a distance, she had always thought that he was cold and hard like his father.

She and Toni had ridden together to a wood on the boundary of their Estates to find the Marquis waiting for them in a little clearing amongst the trees.

Then the expression on his face when he looked at Toni had told Latonia that there was no doubt that he was desperately in love.

When she had taken his hand she had found it firm and she had known it was the handshake of a man who would be both strong and protective.

"Toni has told me how kind you are being to us both," he had said in a deep voice, "and it is difficult for me to thank you or to tell you how grateful I am."

"I want Toni's happiness," Latonia had replied.

"So do I," the Marquis had answered. "But I feel you will understand how impossible it is for me to upset my father when he is so so desperately ill."

They had sat down on a fallen-tree-trunk in the clearing and talked for a long time, and when they left for home, while the Marquis went in the opposite direction, Toni had said eagerly:

"Now, tell me what you think of him!"

"I think he is charming!" Latonia answered. "And, dearest, he is exactly the man I would want you to marry."

Toni had given a little cry of joy.

"I knew you would think that, and, Latonia, I do love him and I will make him a good wife. What is more, I will also be a very good Duchess—not like his toffee-nosed mother was."

"You should not talk like that," Latonia said quickly.

"Because she is dead, I would not say such a thing to Ivan," Toni answered, "but you know as well as I do how disagreeable she was to Mama after the Duke had quarrelled with Papa over the boundaries. When the Queen came to Hampton Towers the Duchess deliberately crossed Mama's name off the list of people who were to be presented to Her Majesty."

"You must forget all that," Latonia said. "It will only upset the Marquis if you keep reminding him of things that happened in the past. Think of the future."

"That is exactly what I intend to do," Toni said, "as long as my future is with him, and that is what it will be—because I love him and he loves me."

It was this which decided Latonia, if she had been undecided before, that she would do everything, however difficult, to ensure that Toni married her Marquis.

At the same time, when they reached London and stopped at the quiet, expensive Hotel where Toni had written to book a room, she felt her heart thumping uncomfortably in her breast and her lips were dry.

However, there was little time to talk, because, as Latonia had half-expected, the Marquis had been horrified at the idea of Toni travelling alone in a Post Chaise all the way back to the country.

"I have now to take a hackney-carriage," Toni said, "to a place just outside London where Ivan will be waiting for me. He will have a closed carriage and no-one will see us when we travel back together to the Manor. From that moment I become Miss Latonia Hythe, while you are the Honourable Latonia Combe, and do not forget it!"

" 'Latonia'?" Latonia questioned.

"Uncle Kenrick always referred to me as 'Latonia' in his letters to Mama and Papa, and I am quite certain he would think 'Toni' far too frivolous a name. So it will not be difficult for you to answer when he speaks to you."

"I am glad you told me," Latonia said. "Oh, please, dearest, before you leave me, think of anything else that I should remember."

"I cannot think of anything to say, except 'thank you' and 'I love you,'" Toni replied. "And do not forget that I have arranged to telegraph you the moment we are married, and then you can come home."

"Yes . . . of course."

"I will make it very discreet so that no-one who is curious will suspect the news is as sensational as it actually is."

"That would be wise," Latonia agreed, "because then I can choose the right moment to tell your uncle the truth."

She shuddered as she spoke, thinking it would be a very difficult and uncomfortable thing to do.

Impulsively she said:

"Oh, please, Toni, hurry up and get married! If I am impersonating you, I shall be going deeper and deeper into a mire of pretence and falsehoods, and I dare not even think of how furious your uncle will be when he finds out I have deceived him."

"He will only be angry with me," Toni said consolingly, "and I shall not be there to hear."

"But I shall!" Latonia murmured, although she knew her cousin was not listening.

They talked for a few more minutes in the Hotel room, then they went downstairs.

Toni, in an authoritative manner, ordered the porters to place the luggage on the hackney-carriage which was to carry Latonia to Branscombe House in Curzon Street.

In the last few days the clothes that Toni wanted

for herself had been conveyed in one way or another to the Manor House.

They were so pretty and at the same time so expensive that Latonia could not help feeling that her small wardrobe would be very surprised to find itself filled with such elegant and fashionable creations rather than the plain, cheap gowns she had made herself with her mother's help.

They also made everything else in the house seem shabby, and it warmed her heart when Toni said enthusiastically:

"I love your little home! I adored coming here as a child, and I feel now that it is just the right place for Ivan and me to be together and talk of our love."

"All I can ask for you in the future, dearest," Latonia said, "is that you will be as happy as Mama and Papa were."

"I used to think when they looked at each other," Toni said, "that their eyes shone like stars, and there was always a note in their voices which was different from the way in which other people talked."

She looked round the room in which they were standing and said quietly:

"I can feel the love they have left behind them and that is the love I shall want in my house and in my life. Otherwise I would rather be an old maid!"

Latonia laughed as she said:

"That is something you will never be!"

"I hope not," Toni replied. "At the same time, if I cannot marry Ivan, I have a feeling I shall never love anybody else in the same way."

She was more serious as she spoke than Latonia had ever remembered her being, and she said quickly:

"But you are going to marry him. Then you will both live happily ever after."

"And if we do, it will be entirely due to our Fairy Godmother—who is you!" Toni said. "Just think of that when Uncle Kenrick is being difficult and raging at you for a lot of sins you have not committed."

"You are frightening me," Latonia said.

37

"There is really no need to be frightened," Toni argued, "because you can leave him as soon as I am married, and then nothing he can say or do can hurt you. He is not your Guardian. He has no jurisdiction over you at all, and once I send you a telegram to say that all is well, you have merely to pack your boxes and come home."

It was Toni who was practical and had remembered that if Latonia was to come home without the help or consent of her uncle, she would need money.

"Here is three hundred pounds, dearest," she had said to Latonia the day before they went to London. "Put it somewhere safely. I am sure there will be thieves on board ship, and certainly in India, if you do not take care of your money."

"I cannot take as much as that!" Latonia had cried.

"You will need it," Toni had insisted, "and remember, because you are so rich, you will be expected to tip more generously than anyone else."

"I shall not know . . . how much to give . . . or when to give it!" Latonia had expostulated.

"You will find out," Toni had replied. "What is more important than anything else is for you to have enough money with which to run away, if Uncle Kenrick is intolerable."

This, Latonia thought now, was consoling, and while she thanked Toni she also thought she would be very careful with the money and on her return would give her back anything that was left over.

"Do not worry about what is happening at the Manor," Toni had said when they drove to London. "I will pay for everything and Ivan will bring me all sorts of delicacies like peaches and grapes."

"You sound as though you are settling down to domesticity," Latonia teased.

"That is exactly what I am doing," Toni answered, "and because I love Ivan so much, I would be perfectly happy with him in a house as small as the Manor. But I do not pretend that later on I shall not enjoy being a Duchess, covering myself in the Hampton diamonds and sitting amongst the Peeresses at the Opening of Parliament."

Latonia laughed.

"Oh, Toni, you always say the unexpected thing, and of course it will be fun to imagine you as a Duchess, just as I want you to be blissfully happy when you marry the Marquis."

"I am greedy—I want it all!" Toni said, and they both laughed.

As they said good-bye to each other, Latonia clung to Toni for a moment as if she could not bear to leave her.

"Thank you, dearest, thank you, thank you!" Toni said. "And Ivan told me yesterday that I was to thank you on his behalf. He is as grateful as I am."

"Think about me ... and pray for me," Latonia said, "because I am so afraid of letting you down."

She drew in her breath before she added:

"Supposing your uncle suspects I am not who I pretend to be, before we even reach the ship?"

"Why should he?" Toni asked. "As you do not look like yourself in that very pretty and expensive bonnet, it is quite obvious you now look like me."

She kissed Latonia.

"Think of it as a story we can tell our grandchildren, and try to get married while you are in India. Then we can race each other by having our babies at the same time, as your mother and mine did."

It sounded so ridiculous that Latonia had to laugh.

She was still smiling as she waved good-bye to Toni, as the hackney-carriage piled with her luggage carried her off to Curzon Street.

As the horse drew up at a very impressive house with a flight of steps leading up to the front door, Latonia knew that the moment had come when she had to meet Toni's uncle and deceive him in a manner in which she had never deceived anybody before in her whole life.

Branscombe House was, she found on entering it, very much the same as the Castle.

Everything was rather heavy and ponderous. The furniture was mostly of mahogany, and the portraits of Branscombe ancestors were just as forbidding as those Toni had known ever since she was a child.

An elderly man-servant led her across the inlaid marble Hall and opened a door at the far end of it.

"Miss Latonia, M'Lord!" he announced in stentorian tones.

Latonia, feeling as if a thousand butterflies were fluttering in her breast, moved forward to where at the end of the room a man was standing in front of the mantelpiece.

She had somehow imagined that the new Lord Branscombe would look very much like his elder brother, whom she had always called "Uncle Hubert."

The first glance told her that she was mistaken.

The man waiting for her as she advanced towards him was taller and more broad-shouldered, with a square-cut face in which Latonia could see no resemblance either to his brother or even, for that matter, to Toni.

As she drew nearer she saw that she was being observed by two steel-grey eyes that looked at her in a penetrating manner which made her see it would be impossible to hide anything from their owner.

She was sure that already he was aware that she was not who she pretended to be.

Then, as it seemed as if she had walked a long way, she reached Lord Branscombe's side and he said in a voice that was cold, authoritative, and at the same time contemptuous:

"You are late! I was expecting you an hour ago!"

The colour rose in Latonia's cheeks as she said a little incoherently:

"I . . . I am sorry . . . Uncle . . . Kenrick . . . but one

of the horses of the carriage in which I was travelling
... cast a shoe ... and I was obliged to ... change to a
hackney-carriage to reach you."

"That is something which should not have happened if your coachman was doing his job!" Lord
Branscombe said sharply.

Latonia felt there was no answer to this.

She merely stood waiting for the next thing he
would say, conscious that they had not shaken hands
and she therefore had not curtseyed to him as she had
intended to do.

"Anyway, you are here," Lord Branscombe remarked, "and I suggest you sit down and listen to
what I have to say to you."

Latonia's eyes had been lowered, and now as she
looked up at him she saw that he was not only still
looking at her with eyes that she felt scrutinised her
critically, but there was also a definite scowl on his
face.

She saw the hard line of his mouth, and she was
sure that if he was incensed because she was late,
there were other reasons as well.

Nervously she sat down on the edge of a chair,
clasping her hands together in their short gloves.

"I think I made it clear in my letter," Lord
Branscombe began, "that the reason I intend taking
you back with me to India is that I can no longer
allow you to behave in the manner you have been
doing since your father's death."

He paused before he continued:

"It is not only Lady Luddington's report of your
disgraceful treatment of her son which has brought
me to this decision, but also various other things I
have heard of your behaviour during the Season when
you were under the chaperonage of your Cousin
Alice."

Because of the way he spoke, Latonia felt a
sudden impulse to defend Toni from accusations
which she could not help feeling came from the
jealousy of other women.

41

Ever since Toni had been fifteen she had not only attracted young men but had also inevitably aroused the jealousy of her own sex.

This came from girls who felt that she outshone them and also from a number of ladies in the County who had sensed that she threatened their security as reigning beauties simply because men of every age found her irresistible.

Aloud she said:

"I do not know what you have ... heard ... but if you are prepared to judge me, I think it only ... fair that you should listen to the defence as well as the ... accusations of the ... prosecution."

She thought Lord Branscombe looked surprised for a moment. Then he replied:

"I have no wish to be involved in arguments, one way or another, but I am quite certain there is no smoke without fire. I therefore consider I am acting in your best interests by taking you away from London."

His lips tightened before he added:

"I hope that by doing so, I can teach you to behave in a more conventional and fitting manner in the future."

He was speaking, Latonia thought, as if he were a very old School-Master berating an unruly pupil.

It was hard to remember that, being fifteen years younger than his elder brother, he could not in fact be more than thirty-four years of age.

'I will not be ... frightened of ... him,' she thought to herself.

At the same time, she knew that she was.

"You may think," Lord Branscombe continued, "that as I am taking you to India you will enjoy the social life which is to be found in Government Houses and wherever there is a group of English people. But that is very far from my intention."

He paused for a moment, then went on:

"If you expect to go to Balls, you will be disappointed. If you are anticipating that you will meet young men who are receptive to your already over-exploited charms, you will find you are mistaken."

His voice sharpened as he continued:

"I have a job to do, and if in accompanying me you see a very different part of the world from what you expect, then perhaps it will be a salutory lesson that in the future you should behave more decorously."

Listening, Latonia thought how angry Toni would have been if she had heard the way he was speaking.

She would undoubtedly have answered him back with a spirited defiance.

Toni would want Balls and certainly the company of young men with whom she could flirt and who would fall in love with her.

If she had not been so frightened, Latonia thought, it was faintly amusing to know that as she wanted none of these things, the punishment that Lord Branscombe was envisaging would not be so severe as he intended.

Because she thought it would surprise him, she said very quietly:

"I shall, as it happens, Uncle Kenrick, be thrilled to see India, and I am not at all worried if I do not have any social life."

She saw Lord Branscombe raise his eye-brows and knew she had been right. This was certainly not the attitude he had expected her to take.

There was a moment's silence, then he said:

"Now that I have made myself clear, I suggest that you go upstairs and rest before dinner. We shall dine early, as we are leaving early in the morning. You will kindly be on time!"

He spoke sharply as if he were speaking to some recalcitrant trooper, and Latonia rose, saying as she did so:

"I will try not to keep you waiting, and thank you for explaining to me your intentions."

43

She made a little curtsey as she spoke, then walked away, conscious, although she did not look round, that the grey eyes were following her, boring into her back.

Only as she reached the Hall, where the Butler was waiting to escort her upstairs, was she aware that her hands were trembling.

Chapter Three

Travelling towards Tilbury, Latonia felt a little surge of excitement at the idea of going abroad.

It had been impossible not to feel extremely apprehensive when at dinner yesterday evening she and Lord Branscombe had sat almost in silence.

She had known, because of the scowl on his face and the manner in which he was looking at her, that he felt both dislike and contempt for her.

It was something she had never encountered before in her happy life, and although she tried to tell herself that it was in fact nothing personal, it did not prevent her from feeling afraid and, though she tried to deny it, upset.

There was something about him which was very overpowering and she thought that Toni must have been right when she said that his Subalterns were afraid of him.

She had tried to make a few commonplace remarks as they were served delicious dishes and waited on by a Butler and two footmen, but Lord Branscombe made very little response and she knew it was because of his disapproval of her—or rather of Toni's —behaviour.

It was as if, as her father would have said, he felt his hackles rise when he looked at her.

"How could anyone feel like this about Toni?" Latonia asked herself.

She thought that if nothing else, she might be

45

able in some way to soften his feelings towards his niece.

When they had finished dinner, which they seemed to hurry through extremely quickly, Lord Branscombe said abruptly:

"I suggest you go to bed and rest. I do not know whether, up to now, you have travelled much, but you will find it tiring, especially if the sea is rough."

"I have no idea whether I am a good sailor or not," Latonia replied. "But I am hoping I will not disgrace myself."

Even as she spoke, she thought that she had given him an opening, and therefore she was not surprised when he made the obvious remark:

"It will certainly not be the first time!"

She wondered what Toni would have said in the circumstances, but when they reached the Hall, Latonia merely curtseyed as she said quietly:

"Good-night, Uncle Kenrick. I will not be late tomorrow morning."

Then she walked up the stairs without looking back.

Breakfast had been brought to her bedroom, and when she came down, wearing an extremely attractive travelling-gown of Toni's covered by a fur-lined cape and a little bonnet trimmed with feathers, she found that Lord Branscombe was already waiting for her.

She was sure that he had his eye on the clock, but as she was three minutes early he could not find fault, and they set off in a comfortable carriage which Latonia knew must have belonged to his brother, as had the horses which drew it.

The Station-Master was waiting to escort them to their reserved compartment and Latonia noticed that there was a Courier who dealt with their luggage, so there was nothing to do except to get into the train, where a number of newspapers and magazines were already laid on their seats.

She wondered if it was only since he had come

into the title that Lord Branscombe travelled in such
luxury, or whether he had been rich enough as an
ordinary soldier to command the same attention.

It was the sort of question she would have liked
to ask him, but she was quite certain that he would
consider it an impertinence. So instead she picked up
one of the magazines.

Lord Branscombe buried himself immediately in
the newspapers, obviously not wishing to talk, and
Latonia was quite happy to watch the countryside
speeding past and to speculate on how exciting it
would be for her to see India.

She thought too that every mile the train carried
them towards Tilbury made it less likely that Lord
Branscombe would guess she was not who she appeared to be, and therefore Toni would be safe with
the Marquis.

She longed to write a letter telling Toni what her
reception had been and what she thought of her
uncle, but it was too dangerous.

Only when she was aboard the ship, Latonia
thought, and there was no chance of her letters being
intercepted, could she write frankly, addressing Toni
of course as "Miss Latonia Hythe."

The black-hulled ship seemed bigger than she
had expected and she learnt that it was one of the
very latest built for the P. & O. line.

The cabins were well furnished and Latonia
found that Lord Branscombe had been allotted a
suite.

Her father had told her that the common abbre-
viation of the best combinations of the cabins, to
avoid the sun, on the India run of the P. & O. was
"Port Outward, Starboard Home," which had gone
into the language as "Posh."

That was what the two cabins, one on either side
of a Sitting-Room, undoubtedly were, and there was
pride in the Purser's voice when he informed His
Lordship that it was the very best accommodation in

the whole ship, usually booked months ahead for their most distinguished and important travellers.

"I am grateful that you could allot it to me at such short notice," Lord Branscombe replied, as was expected of him.

"It's a pleasure, M'Lord," the Purser answered, "and if there is anything you and Miss Branscombe require, I'm at Your Lordship's service."

There was a Stewardess to unpack for Latonia, and as the woman did so she chatted away, telling her that the ship was full.

"You'll have an amusing time, Miss," she added. "There're plenty of young men on board, returning to their Regiments, who will want to dance in the evening, and once we reach the sunshine there'll be deck-games in which I'm sure you'll wish to take part."

"It sounds delightful," Latonia said, "and as I have never travelled on a ship before, I am looking forward to the voyage."

"With these pretty gowns you'll certainly be the 'belle' every evening," the Stewardess said with a smile.

Latonia thought that it sounded amusing and different from what she had expected. She was, however, speedily to be disillusioned.

As there seemed no reason to sit in her cabin while the Stewardess was doing her unpacking, she went into the Sitting-Room and saw that since she had been there before, there had been placed on the table a large number of books and on the writing-desk a huge pile of papers.

She was thinking that Lord Branscombe obviously intended to spend the voyage working, when he came into the cabin.

He had changed from the formal suit he had been wearing for the first part of the journey into what Latonia thought must be a yachting-jacket, which made him look very smart but was not so conventional.

Having looked at her with still the same expression in his eyes as he had before, he said to her sharply:

"Sit down, Latonia. I wish to speak to you."

She obeyed him, wondering what he had to say, and he sat down opposite her, crossing his legs and staring at her reflectively before he began:

"Before we came on this journey I decided to take steps to make sure that you behaved with propriety. Having seen the passengers who are travelling with us and also the programme that has been arranged, I have come to a decision where you are concerned."

Latonia said nothing, she merely looked at him, her eyes very large in her small face.

"I have given orders," Lord Branscombe went on, "that we will eat here in the cabin, and any exercise you take will be in my company, preferably early in the morning or in the evening when the decks are not crowded."

He paused, as if he expected her to say something.

Latonia merely looked at him, thinking as she did so how angry Toni would have been if she had been restricted in such a fashion and made, to all intents and purposes, a prisoner.

As she did not speak, Lord Branscombe continued, almost agressively, as if he thought she wished to argue with him:

"You can hardly expect me to behave in any other manner, considering what I learnt last night."

"What did you learn last night?" Latonia asked.

"I thought that your behaviour with young Luddington was bad enough," Lord Branscombe replied, "but when I was told at my Club of what happened a month ago, I did not believe it possible that any young girl could be not only so outrageous but such a fool."

Latonia felt almost as if he spat the words at her, and after a moment she asked:

49

"What did you ... hear? I do not know what you are talking about."

"You cannot expect me to believe that," Lord Branscombe said sharply. "You must be aware that it was a 'prank,' if that was what you called it, which might have ended in disaster."

Latonia did not reply and he continued:

"Even someone who is half-witted must have known that the currents in the Thames are dangerous, and to invite young men, doubtless bemused by drink, to risk their lives in racing each other across it at night might easily have resulted in one or more of them being drowned."

Latonia drew in her breath, but as Toni had not mentioned this episode to her, there was nothing she could say.

"I do not know who your female accomplices were in this crazy escapade," Lord Branscombe went on, "but I can only imagine that they were as foolish, frivolous, and brainless as you are!"

He paused for a moment before he said:

"All I can say is that you should go down on your knees and thank God that by some miracle newspapers did not get hold of this story, or your reputation would have been more damaged than it is already."

Latonia thought it was not only Toni's reputation which would have been affected if what Lord Branscombe was relating was true, but it was undoubtedly the sort of thing which would have horrified the Duke. It would have made him more sure than he was already that Toni was not the wife he wanted for his son.

She found herself wondering how Toni could have allowed herself to take part in anything so reprehensible, and then she knew it was the kind of fun which her cousin would never have visualised as being wrong.

She imagined it must have been something which had taken place after a dance or a dinner-party, and if the girls had been naughty enough to slip away from their Chaperones, the men had aided and abetted them by suggesting they should take a launch on the river.

It would have seemed romantic on a starlit night, and as there was a whole crowd of them why should Toni have thought it was particularly indiscreet?

Someone might have suggested that it was hot enough to bathe and perhaps another had thought that a swimming-race would be a good idea.

Lord Branscombe might berate Toni for not knowing of the currents in the Thames, but Toni was a country girl.

It would not have occurred to her that the river was any more dangerous than the lake at Branscombe Castle where they had bathed ever since they were children.

As her mother had so often said, they could both swim as if they were fish, and it would never have struck Toni for one moment that grown men might lose their lives swimming in the Thames.

Latonia wondered how she could explain this to Lord Branscombe and then remembered that as Toni was not there, there was really no need to defend her.

He would only think she was making excuses for herself, but at the same time, because he was so angry, she felt her heart beating rather quicker and she said humbly:

"I can only . . . say I am . . . sorry. I did not . . . think it was . . . wrong, but as you said . . . it seemed . . . fun."

"Fun!" Lord Branscombe exclaimed. "When I hear that one man nearly drowned! I was told that it was with the greatest difficulty his friends managed to get him ashore."

"I think perhaps you have been given an . . . exaggerated account of what . . . really happened," Latonia said hesitatingly.

"I can only hope so," Lord Branscombe answered, "but because I feel I cannot trust you out of my sight, I intend to make quite sure that this sort of 'fun,' as you call it, does not happen again."

"I can only ... promise that I will do my ... best not to make you ... angry."

"Angry is not the right word!" Lord Branscombe exclaimed. "I am appalled! Utterly appalled at the damage you have done, not only to young Luddington, whom I have met and liked, but also to a number of other men who have been stupid enough to offer you their hearts and, apparently, their lives to play with."

There was silence and after a moment Latonia said in a hesitating little voice:

"I ... suppose it has never ... struck you that it is not ... entirely my ... fault."

As she spoke, she was thinking how the boys whom they had known when they were young had been bemused and infatuated with Toni from the moment they saw her, long before she made any effort to attract them.

"What do you mean, it is not your fault?" Lord Branscombe asked sharply.

"Just what I say," Latonia answered. "I think that many of the ... young men were not really ... serious in their protestations of ... affection."

"You do not call it serious when a man tries to kill himself?" Lord Branscombe demanded.

Latonia hesitated a moment.

She thought that if she was sensible she would say nothing, for, as Toni had told her to remember, while he ranted at her she had no need to feel that it had anything to do with her personally.

Then, as if she felt his attitude was unfair, she could not resist saying:

"Surely a man who behaved in such an ... exaggerated ... over-emotional manner must be somewhat ... unbalanced."

She spoke very quietly, chosing her words with care, which seemed to infuriate Lord Branscombe.

"How dare you try to shake off your responsibility!" he thundered. "Of course it is your fault if he is driven to such extremes. You must have encouraged him! You must have led him to believe you were interested in him as a man, and then when you had amused yourself at his expense, you threw him off heartlessly and with such cruelty that he lost control of himself!"

"I think," Latonia said, as he obviously was waiting for her to reply, "that you are guessing at what occurred. All I can tell you is that Andrew Luddington made a nuisance of himself to the point when it was impossible for me to . . . tolerate him any longer."

As she spoke, she felt that she must defend Toni and that it was not fair that her uncle should judge her after learning what had hapened from Lady Luddington, who was obviously prejudiced.

"All I can reply," Lord Branscombe said, "is that you are even more heartless than I anticipated, and I am ashamed, bitterly and completely ashamed, that you are my niece."

He walked out of the cabin as he spoke, slamming the door behind him.

Latonia stood for some time, waiting for the turmoil within her to subside and for the fear which had risen in her throat to fade.

'It was stupid of me to argue,' she thought. 'I have only made him . . . dislike Toni more than he does . . . already! But he is unfair! I know he is unfair, and that is something Papa always hated.'

She wished desperately that her father was with her and could tell her what he thought of Lord Branscombe.

He had often accused her of making up her mind too quickly about people and not considering their point of view as well as her own.

"There are always extenuating circumstances for everything people do," he had said.

However, she found it difficult to believe that there could be any extenuating circumstances to account for the manner in which Lord Branscombe was prepared to believe everything that was horrid and unpleasant about his niece and would not give her any chance to excuse herself.

'He is cruel,' Latonia thought.

She told herself that she would be very glad when she was released from her pretended role and could go home.

But as that was something she could not do, she must try now to ignore Lord Branscombe's jibes and accusations and instead enjoy both the voyage and India when they reached it.

At the same time, she knew it was going to be very difficult not to be vividly aware of her supposed Guardian every minute of the day, especially if they were to be cooped up together in the small cabin.

"How can he be so ridiculous," she asked herself, "as to think he could keep someone like Toni confined here and prevent her from mixing with any of the other passengers?"

She knew that Toni would have gone mad at the idea and that somehow, in some mischievous manner of her own, she would have escaped.

She would have bribed the Stewardess, climbed through the portholes—done anything rather than let her uncle succeed in subduing her and keeping her prisoner.

Yet Latonia knew that she herself was not brave enough to defy him, and the small effort she had made to present Toni's point of view had only made him angrier than he was already.

'I must be quiet and accept whatever he says,' she thought.

The ship was still in smooth water, having not yet reached the Channel, and she rose to stand at the table looking at the books. They were all on India and she saw that several were written in what she thought must be Urdu.

Suddenly she had an idea.

About an hour later Lord Branscombe returned to the cabin, looking, she thought, almost as angry as when he had left it.

He did not speak to her and she said tentatively:

"I have something to ask you, Uncle Kenrick."

"What is it?" Lord Branscombe enquired in an uncompromising tone.

"If I am to be kept in here during the voyage; would it be possible for me to learn . . . Urdu?"

She realised that it was the first time she had genuinely surprised him.

"Learn Urdu? Why should you wish to do that?"

"I am very interested in languages," Latonia answered, "and it seems a pity that if I am going to India I shall not to be able to understand what the Indians say."

"A great number speak English," Lord Branscombe replied, "and very few British bother to speak to the natives, who do not understand them."

"I have never had any difficulty in learning European language," Latonia persisted, "and I am sure there must be a teacher of some sort on board. I would like to speak Urdu and I see you have some books here in that language which might be helpful."

"How do you know it is Urdu?" Lord Branscombe asked sharply.

"I thought it . . . must be," Latonia replied after a moment's hesitation.

It had not been possible for her to tell him that when her father was going out to stay in India he had said:

"I am going to have to 'mug up' my Urdu. It will be very rusty after all these years."

"Did you speak it when you were in India?" Latonia had asked him.

"I was very young when I went out with the Regiment. In fact it was my very first appointment as

55

a Subaltern," her father had replied. "As I was full of ambition to get on, I studied Urdu before I left England and during the voyage."

He had laughed as he added:

"I found that such industry was really unnecessary. None of the other Subalterns could speak a word of Urdu, nor did they have any intention of doing so."

"Did it ever come in useful?" Latonia had asked.

"In fact it did," her father had replied. "I found I could talk with Indians in a way which gave me an insight into their characters, and I think the men who served in my Company trusted and respected me, because when they were troubled they could tell me, in their own language, what was wrong."

"They adored your father," Latonia's mother had interposed.

Her husband had smiled at her and she had added:

"If your Regiment had stayed in India instead of coming home, where everything was so much more expensive, I know you would never have left it."

"I think that is true," Captain Hythe had replied. "At the same time, I have no regrets. I have been very happy here at the Manor and the climate would not have been good for Latonia. Children never seem to thrive in the heat."

"That is so," Latonia's mother had said in a soft voice, "and I cannot bear to think of all those little graves in the English cemeteries. The mortality amongst little children is horrifying."

"But we have our Latonia," Captain Hythe had said, putting his arm round his daughter.

Latonia felt now that her father would have wanted her to learn Urdu. So, despite what she felt was Lord Branscombe's scepticism, she persisted.

"Please, can you arrange for someone to teach me? I promise you I will study very hard."

He looked at her suspiciously, as if he thought she had an ulterior motive in wishing to learn an

Indian language, but because there was no reason why she should not do so, he said:

"I will speak to the Purser and see what he can suggest. If not, I suppose I shall have to teach you myself."

"So you have taken the trouble to learn it?" Latonia said.

He did not answer and she had the impression that it was something he did not wish to discuss with her.

It struck her for the first time that as he had said he was going to parts of India where there were no entertainments and perhaps no English people, he must be on some special mission.

She glanced towards the papers on his desk and was certain that the key to what she wanted to know would be amongst them.

After a moment she said:

"You are not joining your Regiment. Now that you have become Lord Branscombe, will you leave the Army?"

There was a frown between his eyes which told Latonia that he did not wish to answer this question either, but at the same time he did not like to refuse to do so.

"I have not yet made any hasty decision," he answered. "I have in fact been requested by the Viceroy to make some investigations which require my travelling to somewhat obscure parts of the country which are off the beaten track."

"That sounds exciting," Latonia said, "and I shall look forward to seeing them."

He looked at her in a way which told her that he thought she was just being pleasant for reasons of her own and would not genuinely wish to do anything that did not involve the entertaining, the dancing, and the other amusements which he knew had been her sole interest while in London.

"Please, will you tell me about your investigations?" Latonia asked.

Almost as if he was embarrassed, Lord Branscombe walked to his desk to look at the papers on it
before he said:

"I have undertaken to enquire into the behaviour
and political inclinations of certain small States which
at the moment do not have a British Resident. I
presume you know what that means?"

"Yes, of course," Latonia replied. "British Resi-
dents are appointed to guide and advise the Princes or
Rajahs and also to prevent any forbidden customs like
Suttee from taking place."

As she spoke, she thought that Lord Branscombe
was surprised that she should know about *Suttee*,
which was the burning of a man's wives with his
corpse when he died.

"I think that is a pretty good summary of the
duties of a British Resident," he conceded, "but as you
can imagine, the Princes make every effort to do
without them."

"So when you make your investigations you will
not be very welcome," Latonia said with a faint
smile.

"That is true," Lord Branscombe agreed. "At the
same time, I am not particularly interested in what
people feel about me personally. I must do my duty
whether they like it or not!"

Latonia thought that this was rather the attitude
he was taking up with regard to Toni, but aloud she
said:

"Perhaps when you have time you will show me
on the map where we will be travelling, as I would
like, if possible, to read a little beforehand about the
different places we shall visit, so that I shall not miss
anything when we are there."

She thought Lord Branscombe looked unrespon-
sive and she went on:

"And please, will you enquire about Urdu lessons
as soon as possible? It will be difficult to learn much
in such a short time, but at least I can make a

beginning. And when I reach India I shall be able to talk to the servants."

"I am not sure that would be advisable," Lord Branscombe said sharply.

"Then of course you will have to tell me, Uncle Kenrick, to whom I can talk and with whom I must keep silent," Latonia said.

Again she thought he was suspicious because she was being so amenable.

Then finally he took from amongst his papers a small book which she saw, when he put it down on the table in front of her, was a dictionary of Urdu words.

"Pull up a chair at the table and I will see," he said, "if you have an ear for learning what is a difficult language which requires a great deal of concentration. If I think it is hopeless from the start, I will say so, and you must accept my decision in this matter."

"But of course," Latonia agreed. "I quite understand, and I am very grateful. At the same time, I do not wish to be a nuisance, since I can see you have brought a great deal of work with you. Would it not be better to find me a teacher?"

"It may be possible later, I do not know," Lord Branscombe replied. "First we have to establish if you are teachable."

"Yes, of course," Latonia said. "It will be very humiliating if I prove to be as half-witted as you think I am."

As she spoke, she thought that she was being very brave in speaking in such a manner to Lord Branscombe. At the same time, she could not help feeling extremely resentful that he had been so unkind about Toni.

No-one knew better than Latonia that although Toni might be frivolous and might at times do foolish things, she actually had a sharp brain and was much more intelligent than most girls of her age.

She was not in fact as clever as Latonia was

herself, for the simple reason that she found it difficult to settle down to one subject for any length of time or to concentrate as Latonia did on any subject which particularly interested her.

Latonia had always had time to read because there had not been so many diversions at the Manor as there had been at the Castle.

She had been brought up without spirited horses to ride, without many broad acres as a playground, without a lake in which to swim, and without a huge Castle packed with treasures of every sort and description.

This meant that Latonia was thrown back on her own resources, and she had learnt to use her imagination and to apply it to everything she read in books.

Both her father and her mother had been very intelligent people, and between them, because they loved their only child and she was always with them, they had educated her without her really being aware of it.

Because neither of them was interested in the gossip and the chatter with which most people filled their lives, they talked on almost every subject that had concerned mankind since the beginning of time —subjects which embraced the developments of civilisation and concerned both this world and the next.

Sometimes Toni would get impatient when Latonia would spend a long time in the Library at the Castle, looking for some particular book she wanted.

"Oh, come on, Latonia," she would say, "the horses are waiting. Why must you waste the sunshine?"

"I am trying to find a book about the Roman Conquest, which Papa and Mama were talking about last night," Latonia would reply.

Or else it would be the building of the Taj Mahal, the Hanging Gardens of Babylon, or the Light-House at Alexandria.

To Latonia, what she wished to read was an

extension of something which had captured her imagination.

It had seemed very real to her when her father and mother talked about it, and, by wishing to know more, she had taught herself in a way that no teacher could have managed to do.

She knew now, as Lord Branscombe sat down opposite her with what she thought was bad grace, that he was quite convinced that her interest in India was only superficial, or perhaps just a desire to ingratiate herself with him so as to placate his anger over other things.

Because her imagination was incited by the very first words he said and because she genuinely wished to learn, it was a long time later when he shut the book and said:

"I think you have done enough for today. You certainly show a natural aptitude for languages, which I had not expected."

"It is so interesting!" Latonia exclaimed. "And I can see now how quite a number of Indian words have grown into the European languages."

She did not notice that Lord Branscombe looked surprised as she went on:

"I always thought that the Gypsy Romany language came from the Hindu and now I am sure of it."

"Are you telling me that you speak Romany?" Lord Branscombe enquired.

Latonia smiled at him.

"Not well," she answered, "because, as you know, Gypsies are very diffident about letting anyone know their language. But since they have camped in the Park—your Park—every year, I have known them since I was a child and I have picked up enough of their language to be able to greet them and ask after their health."

"You surprise me," Lord Branscombe said. "I am even more surprised that my brother should have allowed you to speak to the Gypsies, let alone associate with them."

There was just a faint twinkle in Latonia's eyes as she replied:

"I do not think he was always aware of my friendship with the travelling-people."

She had a feeling that she had said the wrong thing, for immediately the frown was back between Lord Branscombe's eyes and he said sharply:

"You appear to have spent your life steeped in intrigue. I can assure you, if I ever have children I shall bring them up extremely strictly."

Latonia wondered if she should have replied that that was exactly the way his brother had tried to bring up Toni.

It was not only because he and Toni's mother wanted her to be a good child but because they were afraid for her.

They always wanted to keep her under their eye and to prevent her from doing anything in which she might harm herself or hear anything she should not hear.

Because Miss Waddesdon had been more lenient, Toni and she had been able to do a thousand things which Lord and Lady Branscombe would have vetoed immediately, had they been aware of what was happening.

What Latonia had been thinking must have shown in her expression, for after a moment Lord Branscombe said:

"I can sense that you do not agree with me, which is not surprising."

"I think that children, like most people," Latonia said slowly, "if they are categorically forbidden to do one particular thing, look upon it as forbidden fruit."

"And what is the alternative?"

"I should think that is obvious!" she replied. "If you tell a child reasonably that something is wrong or dangerous, convince him or her that that is why it is forbidden, then there is much more likelihood that

you will be obeyed than if you just give peremptory
orders which anyone with spirit would resent."

"Is that what happened to you?" Lord Branscombe enquired.

Latonia almost replied that her parents had been
so broad-minded that she always felt she was given
the choice of what she might do and not do. Then she
remembered that she was pretending to be Toni.

"Yes, that is exactly what did happen," she replied. "I seem to remember ever since I was a small
child being told 'No, no!' instead of 'Yes, yes!' "

"So, what you are saying," Lord Branscombe said,
as if he was reasoning it out, "is that when you were
grown up, whenever you had the chance you deliberately did things you knew were wrong . . ."

"Not deliberately," Latonia interrupted, "but I
suppose that like everyone else I wanted to be free to
stretch my wings, to prove that I was a person, not
just a puppet manipulated by strings."

"I cannot believe that such an assertion has any
foundation of fact," Lord Branscombe said sharply.

"You know what . . . Papa was . . . like," Latonia
replied, talking as if she were Toni. "He never put a
foot wrong from the time he was a little boy. He
wanted his life to be ordered on the rigid lines that it
always had followed in his father's time and his
grandfather's before that. Surely . . . you felt that
when you were . . . small and . . . living at home?"

"I suppose that is true," Lord Branscombe said,
as if he thought of it now for the very first time.

There was silence while Latonia was certain that
he was thinking over what she had said and assimilat-
ing it. Then suddenly he said sharply:

"You are making a very good case for yourself,
Latonia, but do not think that you can blind me by
argument or make me change my mind about what I
am going to do with you and how I intend you will
behave now that I have taken over the job of Chaperone."

"I am not arguing," Latonia answered, "I am

only showing you perhaps a different angle from the one from which you have contemplated the subject previously."

"I am not concerned with angles," Lord Branscombe replied. "As far as you are concerned, I wish you to keep to the path of righteousness and I intend that is what you will do."

Latonia smiled at him.

"As long as the path leads to India and the learning of Urdu, I am for the moment perfectly content."

She knew by the way he moved sharply away from the table to sit down at his desk that he was a little discomfited by her answer.

"Now," he said, "I intend to concentrate on my own work, which is something I must not neglect."

"Then I will not disturb you," Latonia answered sweetly, "and thank you so much for all you have taught me so far. I shall do my best not to forget it, and I hope to have learnt a great many more words before you give me my second lesson."

As she went to her own cabin, she had the satisfaction of thinking that she was surprising Lord Branscombe in accepting his punishment in a way which he had not expected.

"I hate him for the way he is determined to be so unkind to Toni," she told herself.

At the same time, he was obviously as clever as she had always heard he was, and she was determined to pick his brains in one way or the other!

She smiled as she thought how amused Toni would be if she knew what was happening.

She told herself that she would start this very evening to write a long letter to her cousin, which she would post at their first port-of-call.

At least what was happening was exciting. It was certainly very different from the kind of life she had had ever since she had been in mourning for her father and mother and Toni had gone to London.

Then nothing had happened from day to day. So,

to Latonia, although Lord Branscombe was not aware of it, everything, even being confined to her cabin, was an adventure.

'I will really try hard with my Urdu, if only because it will annoy him,' Latonia thought. 'He is so determined to prove me, or rather Toni, to be a half-wit and it will be a real score if I can make him eat his words!'

Then it struck her that perhaps the reason he was so disagreeable and upset by Toni was that he was a woman-hater.

This was a new idea, and as Latonia sat thinking it over, she told herself that perhaps the reason he was so incensed about Andrew Luddington was that he himself had been thrown over by some attractive girl and it had made him suspicious and cynical where all women were concerned.

With his handsome looks and his distinguished career, there must have been a great number of women in his life, in one way or another.

Latonia could not remember her father or her mother or anyone at the Castle speaking of Kenrick Combe in a romantic fashion.

They had always talked of his achievements in the Regiment, the distinctions which were poured upon him, and the complimentary letters that Lord Branscombe had received about his brother.

'Perhaps he has never loved anyone,' Latonia thought.

But she was sure that there had been women who had loved him.

'What is his secret?' she wondered, and felt certain that there was one.

This was something else which could occupy her imagination, and she thought with a lift of her heart that because there was a mystery about Lord Branscombe, he did not seem quite so awe-inspiring and frightening as he had done previously.

Chapter Four

Latonia tossed and turned on her bed and found it impossible to sleep once they had passed through the Suez Canel and into the Red Sea.

It had become almost unbearably hot and she found herself longing all through the day to be up on deck and hoping that there would be a cool breeze blowing under the awning.

But Lord Branscombe had set a pattern for their days from which she thought that even a typhoon would be unable to dislodge him.

They walked round at seven o'clock in the morning, before breakfast, keeping to the top deck where it was less likely that there would be other passengers.

The people they did see were either not attractive or, Latonia thought, not interested in them. But she felt all the time that in his self-appointed rule as jailor Lord Branscombe watched her, expecting her to do something outrageous, although she had no idea what it could be.

After breakfast he usually spent two hours teaching her Urdu. He was extremely punctilious about it, and at the same time impersonal in a way which she found hard to describe even to herself.

She was quite sure that there must be someone on board capable of teaching a pupil who was only at the primary stage of learning a language, but Lord Branscombe, having once said that he would be her

66

teacher, was determined not to delegate his authority.

What Latonia found very disconcerting was that she was quite sure he found it an unpleasant, boring task because he disliked her so much.

As she had never been with anyone in her life who had an aversion for her, she found it hard, day after day, not to break down and ask him to be a little kinder and a little more human.

But she knew that not only would he refuse any request that she might make, but he would think he had achieved his object if she admitted to any weakness.

He was punishing her—that was obvious—and for a punishment to be effective the offender must become humble and repentant. But that, Latonia told herself with pride, was something which she had no intention of being.

She was quite certain that if Toni had been there, by this time she and her uncle would have been at daggers-drawn. They would have raved at each other and Toni would have behaved badly simply to defy him.

Latonia was determined to be conciliatory but not humble. She agreed with everything Lord Branscombe suggested, and she did so with what she thought was a quiet dignity.

Once or twice she thought she saw an expression of surprise in his eyes, but she was not certain. In fact, she told herself, he was an enigma and it was very hard to know what he was feeling about her or about anyone else.

After their lesson he would usually rise from the table and sit at his desk to work on his papers, about which she had become extremely curious. But she was sure he would think it an impertinence if she questioned him about them.

When alone in the cabin she had been tempted to look at his papers and find out for herself, but then she thought it would be disgraceful to spy on him, even though under the same circumstances he would spy on her.

She had the feeling that he was longing to trip her up, watching her as if she were a wild animal which might make a break for freedom at any moment.

In the evenings she spent the time reading, and as fortunately it was something she enjoyed, she usually became completely absorbed in her book.

It was by no means a penance to curl up on the sofa in the cabin and read one of the many books on India which she had discovered were obtainable from the ship's Library.

A Steward had brought her a catalogue of what they had, and she had chosen half-a-dozen books on her own initiative before Lord Branscombe was aware of what she was doing.

"Where have these come from?" he asked one morning.

They had returned from their pre-breakfast walk to find a whole pile of books on the side-table in the cabin.

"They are from the Library," Latonia explained. "I asked a Steward to obtain them for me."

"You might have consulted me first," he replied, looking at the books." I should have been able to advise you which would be worth reading."

"I could not be sure that your taste is the same as mine," Latonia said with a faint smile.

He looked at her sharply, as if he thought she was being rude. Then, turning over the books in what she thought was a disdainful fashion, he was forced, against every inclination, to admit that there was nothing wrong with her choice.

"I will see what else is available," he said, "but I imagine these will take you some time to get through."

"I am a very quick reader."

"And you are really interested in India?"

"I should have thought you would have realised

that by this time, and that is why I am so keen to learn Urdu."

There was nothing he could say to that, because she was aware that he had been surprised at how quickly she had picked up a smattering of the language, and she knew that her pronunciation of the words was quite as good as his.

He tried to discourage her from being pleased with herself by telling her that there were very many different languages and dialects in India.

But she remembered her father saying that Urdu was the most common, and she worked hard at improving her vocabulary from the dictionary when Lord Branscombe was busy at his desk.

The heat in the Red Sea made Latonia feel so limp that it was impossible to concentrate on a book or anything else, and she rose from her bed to go to the open porthole.

She looked out and saw that there was just a faint golden light on the horizon which heralded the dawn.

The stars were still twinkling in the sky but she knew that with the swiftness of the coming day, within a few minutes they would begin to fade as the rising fingers of light swept them into oblivion.

"It is so lovely, so beautiful," she told herself, and she had a sudden longing to see more.

Swiftly, without really thinking about it, she dressed and, opening the cabin door, ran down the corridor towards the door which led onto the deck.

A moment later she was at the rail-side, and as she watched the light growing and expanding on the horizon and felt a cool breeze blowing against her skin, she knew it was what she had longed for.

Then she was spellbound as the sun, suddenly dazzling in her eyes, turned the sea to a glittering glory which seemed to ripple from the horizon towards the ship.

"It is a wonder beyond words," Latonia said to herself and felt as if the glory of it became part of her heart.

The sun rose higher and now she moved towards the stern, anxious to get away from the door through which she had come on deck in case anyone saw her.

She reached the end of the rail where she could look down on the lower deck, where some of the steerage-class passengers sat most of the day. Their cabins were small and airless and, as the ship was full, exceedingly cramped.

At the moment it was too early for anyone to be about except several men who had obviously slept on deck and were still lying in a recumbent position.

Latonia stood looking astern.

The ship made green and white waves as it moved through the calm water, and she knew that in a little while the sun would be so hot that she must either fetch a hat or move under the awning.

Suddenly she was aware that two people had joined her at the rail. One was a very old man and with him was a middle-aged woman wearing a uniform which proclaimed her to be a Nurse.

They stood looking at the sea as Latonia was, then suddenly the Nurse said:

"I wonder, Miss, if you'd look after him for a moment. I feel sick, not from the sea but from something I ate last night."

"Yes, of course," Latonia replied.

She thought as she spoke that the woman had a green look about her, as if she had in fact been poisoned.

The Nurse hurried away with a speed which showed her urgency, and Latonia moved closer to the old man, who was holding on to the rail with his blue-veined hands.

"Pretty," he said, as if he was speaking to himself. "Very—pretty."

"Yes, it is," Latonia agreed. "The sun makes us all feel happy."

She spoke quietly, but he turned his head to look at her and asked in a frightened voice:

"Where—is my—Nurse? Where has she—gone?"

"She is coming back in a moment," Latonia said soothingly. "She will not be more than a minute or two."

"I want her!" the old man said crossly. "I—want her! She has—left me—alone!"

"She is coming back," Latonia repeated, but he was obviously as agitated as a child might be at losing what was familiar.

He took his hands from the rail and turned unsteadily. Latonia thought he was going to fall and quickly she put one hand in his and her other arm round his shoulders to steady him.

"Your Nurse will be back in a moment," she said, "and you must tell her how pretty the sea is."

It was either the tone of her voice or perhaps the touch of her hand which reassured him. His fingers tightened on hers, and as Latonia drew him back to the rail he put out his other hand to hold on to it.

Latonia kept her arm round him, thinking that he might still make an effort to go seek his Nurse. He was very old and frail.

"Look at the sunshine on the waves," she suggested softly.

Then suddenly she heard the sharp voice of Lord Branscombe ask:

"What the devil do you think you are doing here?"

She turned her head without relinquishing her hold on the old man and found that he was just behind her. There was no doubt of the expression of anger and suspicion on his face.

"So I cannot even trust you not to sneak out while I am asleep," he said furiously. "Who is this man?"

He was not able to see the old man's face because, as Latonia had told him to, he was watching the sunshine on the sea.

All Lord Branscombe could see was that Latonia had her arm round a man's shoulder and her hand in his.

71

If he had not taken her by surprise and if in fact she had not felt agitated by the anger in his voice, she might have thought it amusing.

As it was, for the moment she could only stare at him, finding it hard to believe that anyone would be so suspicious of what had been on her part nothing but an act of charity.

Then as she realised what he was thinking and knew of what he was accusing her, the Nurse came back.

The Nurse moved to the other side of the old man, saying as she did so:

"Thank you ever so much, Miss, for looking after him. I hope he's been no trouble."

"You're—back," the old man said in his quavering voice. "Why did you—go away? I—thought I had—lost you."

"You won't do that," the Nurse said cheerily. "Come on, put your arm through mine and we'll go walkies. You know the Doctor said you were to move about."

As he put his arm through the Nurse's, Latonia relinquished her hold on him. The Nurse and the old man moved away and she turned round to face Lord Branscombe, who was still standing a little behind her.

She looked up at him, her head silhouetted against the glory of the sun. There was no need for words, and after a moment, when his eyes held hers, he said:

"I suppose I should apologise?"

"I think that . . . would be the . . . fair thing to . . . do."

Lord Branscombe moved to the rail and leant over it.

"You can hardly expect me to be anything but suspicious, considering the stories I have been told about you in the past."

It was as if he wished to excuse himself for his own hasty judgement, but Latonia replied:

"I believe in a Court of Law they will not admit hearsay as evidence."

She thought for one moment there was just a faint smile at the corners of Lord Branscombe's lips, before he answered:

"There is also such a thing as circumstantial evidence."

"Which still has to be proved," Latonia said quickly.

There was silence. Then Lord Branscombe said:

"I suppose you would consider it right and proper, or shall I say 'fair,' if I listen to any explanations you might wish to make."

Latonia looked out over the sea before she said:

"We are moving towards a part of the world I have never visited before and we have left England behind. Surely we can do the same about my past."

"Is that what you want to do, or is that a statement which you think will impress me?"

She had a feeling which she could not substantiate, that he was deliberately forcing himself into being more disagreeable than he actually felt.

"I have just watched the dawn of a new day," Latonia said. "Perhaps human beings have new dawns in their lives? If Nature can be born anew, cannot we?"

"That is an idea which has never occurred to me," Lord Branscombe replied, "for the simple reason that medically it is not accepted."

"Then perhaps I can be the exception," Latonia said. "I want to think that the past is no longer important, it is the . . . future which . . . matters."

She meant to speak lightly, but somehow her voice sounded serious and almost as if it was a plea.

He turned to look at her, and because he was looking at her penetratingly, critically, the blood rose in her cheeks. After a moment he said:

"You surprise me, Latonia. In fact I have been continually surprised by you ever since we met."

"Why?"

"Because you are not what I expected."

Latonia had no wish to reply and she could not help a little tremor of fear in case he was being remarkably perceptive and had guessed that she was not who she pretended to be.

Then, as if he wished to find fault, Lord Branscombe said in a different tone of voice:

"Why did you break the rules and come on deck so early?"

"I could not sleep because it was so hot," Latonia replied. "I also wanted to see the dawn. The moment before the sun rises is so breathless, so exciting, that it is something I will always remember."

"You will see many beautiful dawns while you are in India," Lord Branscombe said in a different voice, "especially near the Himalayas."

Latonia clapped her hands together.

"Is that where we are going?"

"Eventually."

"That is what I have longed for, prayed for . . . that one day I should see the Himalayas."

"Why?"

There was silence while she tried to find words to answer.

"They have always been to . . . me in my . . . imagination, not only the most beautiful mountains in the world . . . but perhaps a . . . symbol of man's endeavour to reach beyond himself towards God."

She did not realise that Lord Branscombe looked at her almost incredulously as she went on:

"That is what I . . . feel they mean to the . . . Indian people and perhaps to all those who through the . . . ages have sought to . . . pierce the veil between this world and the next."

Latonia had spoken almost as though she was speaking to herself.

She was thinking out her own answer to his question, finding it difficult to choose the right words to express her inner feelings, yet determined to give them their full meaning.

There was a long silence and she thought that perhaps Lord Branscombe would go on with the conversation.

She had, for the first time, the feeling that he knew a great deal more about what she was trying to say than she knew herself.

She wanted to question him and she wanted him to explain so much which she found bewildering.

Then abruptly, almost as if he called himself to attention, he said:

"It is really a little early for our walk, but I think we should go up on the top deck for our exercise."

* * *

When the *Odessa* steamed into Bombay Harbour on the seventeenth day after they had left England, Latonia thought it was the most exciting thing that had ever happened to her.

Her enthusiasm and excitement had forced Lord Branscombe on deck far earlier than he had intended, and as he stood looking at the mist which hung over the great Harbour there was a bored expression on his face.

But, despite this, Latonia had the feeling that he was not so blasé and uninterested as he tried to pretend.

Latonia had hoped that she would have time to see the town, but when they went ashore Lord Branscombe had been met by a number of Army Officers, and, having retrieved their luggage and been shown into a carriage driven by soldiers in uniform, they set off immediately for the railway-station.

Latonia just had time to see the massive parade of huge official buildings built parallel to the sea and separated from the beaches only by an expanse of brownish turf, a railway-line, and a riding-track.

It was all very different from what she had expected, yet as Lord Branscombe pointed out to her the Secretariat, the University, the Library, the Law

Courts, and the Post-Office, she thought they had a familiar look in that they could be nothing but the creation of the British.

She did not say so, as she thought it might sound as if she was being critical, but when they reached the railway-station she found it the grandest of all the buildings, mock-Oriental, Saracenic, Moghul with domes, clocks, and stained-glass windows.

Here the threatrical confusion of the platforms was exactly what she had expected, a frenzy of Indians in turbans, priestly yellow robes, nose-clips, loin-cloths, and *dhotis*.

While the huge engines steamed and hissed, hawkers shouted their wares and beggars with mutilated faces or twisted limbs made their whining voices heard.

However, there was little time for Latonia to enjoy the colourful confusion.

The Officers who had met Lord Branscombe on the ship had followed them in another carriage and were now waiting to escort them to the train.

As a concession to His Lordship's importance they had a sleeping-coach, a Drawing-Room, and a servants' compartment attached to the original train, which was filled to suffocation.

Lord Branscombe had introduced Latonia in a perfunctory way to the Officers who had met him, and now as she joined them in the Drawing-Room she was aware that two of the younger men looked at her with a glint of admiration in their eyes.

"I hope you will enjoy India, Miss Combe," one of them said. "You will find plenty of gaiety in Simla, if your uncle is taking you there."

"I am not certain where we are going," Latonia replied.

The Officer looked surprised before he said:

"Well, I hope for your sake that it will be one of the Hill Stations, but I am certain you will also find an enthusiastic welcome waiting for you in Delhi."

Latonia thought it strange that Lord Branscombe,

after their first conversation in which he had told her that she could enjoy none of the entertainments and amusements of India, had never mentioned their destination again.

It suddenly struck her that perhaps it was secret, though why he should be moving about in such a manner she had no idea.

There was still some time before the train left, when Lord Branscombe said unexpectedly:

"I think, Latonia, it would be a good idea if you saw that everything you require for the journey has been placed in your bedroom. The rest of your luggage will be in the van."

She knew quite well that what he was saying was that he wished her to leave the Drawing-Room.

She rose from the chair in which she had been sitting and held out her hand to the young Officer with whom she had been talking.

"Good-bye."

He held her hand a little longer than was necessary.

"Good-bye," he answered, "and I hope we shall meet again, Miss Combe."

"I hope so too," she replied.

She smiled at him as she would have smiled at anyone who had been talking to her politely.

But she had the uncomfortable feeling that Lord Branscombe was glaring at her, and as she walked away towards her own compartment, which adjoined the Drawing-Room, she thought it could be intolerable that anytime she spoke to a man, he suspected her of behaving badly.

'What can Toni have done,' she wondered as she had wondered a thousand times before, 'to make him feel like this about her?'

There was, of course, the attempted suicide of Andrew Luddington, but, although that was a terrible thing to have happened, Latonia felt he must have been a weak, rather stupid character, and a man who had commanded troops would surely realise this.

"Perhaps Lord Branscombe believes what he wants to believe," she told herself.

When she reached her compartment she found, as she had expected, that the luggage she wanted was there and there was no reason for her to worry about it.

She raised the blind over the window and looked out at the seething crowds on the platform, dazzled by the kaleidoscope of colour.

She thought that the women in their saris and the children with their huge dark eyes and their small, olive-skinned faces were very beautiful.

After she had watched everything for some time, she decided that she would go back to the Drawing-Room even if Lord Branscombe did not want her.

Toni undoubtedly would have resented being sent away like an unwanted parcel, and because Latonia was determined to show her independence she decided to return.

She opened the door into the Drawing-Room and as she did so she heard the Officer who was the senior of those who had met Lord Branscombe say:

"For God's sake, Branscombe, take every precaution. As you are well aware, these small independent States will do anything to prevent their behaviour coming to the notice of the Viceroy. If they think you are a threat, they will undoubtedly try to dispose of you in one way or another."

Latonia stood listening and felt that what she was hearing could not be true but must be a figment of her imagination.

It was too like an adventure-story from a Boys' Paper, and yet the Officer had undoubtedly said the words she had just heard.

There was in his voice an inescapable note of sincerity as well as one of warning. Then she heard Lord Branscombe laugh.

"I can take care of myself, Stevens, as you must know by this time. On this journey I am in a position of authority, instead of being on an undercover investigation."

"I am aware of that; at the same time, I do beg of you to take care. The last report we had from ..."

He lowered his voice so that it was barely above a whisper and Latonia could not hear any more.

Because she was surprised at what she had overheard, she turned and went back into her own compartment.

Surely, she thought, Lord Branscombe was not taking her, as his niece, into danger?

Yet there was no mistaking what the Officer called Stevens had said, and she had a feeling that he spoke with a knowledge of what lay ahead, while Lord Branscombe, just arriving from England, might be completely ignorant.

"Surely he will listen to him?" Latonia asked herself.

The train started, and because she knew that Lord Branscombe would now be alone she moved quickly into the Drawing-Room.

He was standing at the window, looking at the crowds on the platform, who were staring at the moving train as if it were a prehistoric monster, and Latonia went to his side to say:

"I had never imagined there could be so many people on a platform at one time."

Lord Branscombe smiled.

"Trains in India are both an amusement and a terror to the native population. At the same time, it is something new and they find it too fascinating to miss."

"I can understand that," Latonia said. "And as we are talking about a new world, will you tell me where we are going?"

Lord Branscombe gave her a sharp glance, as if he expected that she had a reason for asking the question, before he replied:

"Is it of any great interest?"

"It is to me," Latonia said, "and as I asked you

before, I would like to have a map to follow our journey on, so that when it is over I can retrace our steps in my imagination."

"I do not have a map at hand," Lord Branscombe replied, "but I daresay I can find you one later."

She had the feeling that he was deliberately prevaricating and avoiding answering her question.

She sat down on a chair, looking at him as she asked:

"Are you in the Secret Service?"

There was a distinct pause before he replied:

"Why should you ask such a question?"

"Perhaps you will think I am perceptive, or it might be better for me to be frank and say that I overheard something which was said to you just now."

Lord Branscombe looked angry and she added quickly:

"I did not intend to eavesdrop. I opened the door and heard an Officer called Stevens begging you to be careful."

"Stevens should be more discreet in what he says," Lord Branscombe replied sharply.

"I would rather know the truth," Latonia insisted. "If we are going into danger, then I, as well as you, will have to look out for it and it is best to be prepared."

Lord Branscombe frowned.

"If there was any real danger," he said, "I should not take you with me. There are plenty of people, friends of mine, who would be only too pleased to chaperone you. But, as you are well aware, I have my reasons for keeping you under my eye and away from the sort of society in which you would inevitably get into trouble."

"I have always believed that one is innocent until one has been proved guilty," Latonia said lightly.

"I have an easy answer to that," Lord Branscombe said, "but I thought we agreed to speak only of the future."

"I have no wish to be put in the charge of a

Chaperone or to be subjected to the temptations of which you are so afraid," Latonia said.

She knew her words brought a scowl to Lord Branscombe's face, but she continued before he could speak:

"I would much prefer to be with you and to visit the places which you say are off the beaten track and different from what most tourists in India see. But I would also like to know what I am in for, and if your life is in danger, then four eyes are better than two."

"You should not have listened to what was not meant for your ears," Lord Branscombe replied sharply, "and you certainly need not concern yourself about the danger of what I am doing. I assure you I shall be perfectly safe, as you will be. If there is any likelihood of anything else, I promise you we shall leave immediately for the nearest British Residency."

Latonia sighed.

"You are deliberately trying not to understand what I am asking of you," she said. "It does sound like an adventure-story and indeed what one would expect of India, and if this is part of the intrigue and the secrecy which I have read is necessary for the running of this great country, then I want to do what I can to help."

She spoke with an unmistakable sincerity and she knew that Lord Branscombe was, almost despite himself, impressed by what she was saying.

Just for a moment she thought he was about to be frank and take her into his confidence, but when he would have replied, two Stewards came into the carriage to tell them that at the next station their luncheon would be brought aboard and they hoped it would be to their liking.

The stops at different stations, the attention they received from their own Stewards, and the fact that Lord Branscombe was obviously determined not to have a confidential talk with her made it difficult for Latonia to do anything but make commonplace remarks for the rest of the day.

At the same time, when she went to bed she found herself increasingly intrigued with the idea that the journey on which she was accompanying Lord Branscombe was one of importance.

She knew that the Viceroy and the network of officials under him ran the country, in which three hundred million people were controlled by what was in proportion a mere handful of British.

Lying awake while the train thundered over the rails, Latonia tried to remember what she had heard of the difficulties in India.

Her father had often spoken of the country but usually it concerned the days when he was there with his Regiment. She had also obtained some information from the books that she had found in the ship's Library.

She had the feeling that the menace of the Russians and their infiltration into Afghanistan somehow concerned Lord Branscombe, and yet she had no grounds for actually thinking so.

'There is so much I want to ask him, so much he could tell me,' Latonia thought, and yet she had the feeling that because he disliked her he did not trust her.

It would be useless to question him.

However, she had a very retentive memory and she knew she had read somewhere—it was not important where—that the Russians were moving East and South, absorbing one after the other the Khans of Central Asia in preparation for the encirclement of India.

It seemed far-fetched, and yet in another book she had read that there was a Russian railway being built across Siberia to the Far East and the rumour of another in Turkistan which might be the beginning of a plan to annexe Tibet.

'If only Lord Branscombe would talk to me,' Latonia thought, and she was determined to force from him an answer to what she wished to know.

The following morning, after their breakfast had been removed, she asked:

"Would you like to explain to me what is happening amongst the Muslim tribes on the frontier between Afghanistan and India?"

There was no doubt that Lord Branscombe stiffened at her question.

"Who have you been talking to?" he asked sharply.

Latonia smiled.

"As you are well aware, I have not had the opportunity of talking to anyone but you, but at least you have allowed me to read."

She thought he relaxed before he said:

"I am sure I can find you some books on the subject, if that is what interests you."

"I would much rather you talked to me and explained what I want to know."

"And what is that?"

"How dangerous are the tribesmen in the North, and are the Prussians deliberately using smaller, independent Princes to further their own interests?"

She had the feeling that if she had dropped a bomb at Lord Branscombe's feet he could not have been more astonished.

At the same time, after an initial start of surprise he appeared relaxed, and, apart from what she thought was a dangerous glitter in his grey eyes, his face was quite expressionless.

"I cannot imagine what book you have read which is full of such nonsense," he said. "I personally think the menace of the Russians has been deliberately blown up out of all importance by writers like Kipling, who want to sell their books."

Latonia did not answer, and after a moment, as if he was curious to know her reaction to his words, he asked:

"Do you believe me?"

She shook her head slowly.

83

"I might have done so," she said, "if I had not heard what Colonel Stevens said to you last night."

Lord Branscombe made an exclamation of impatience and then he said:

"Very well, I can see there might be some truth in the supposition, but that is not the reason for my journey, which is merely to make contact with Princes, to find out if they need British assistance in running their States, and to assure them that their loyalty, if they give it to the British Raj, will be rewarded."

She felt that meagre though the information was, he resented having to give it to her.

She could not help there being just a faint note of triumph in her voice when she replied:

"Thank you so much for telling me. It makes it all the more interesting to know why we are doing something. It would also be more exciting if only I knew where."

Just for a moment she thought Lord Branscombe might rage at her, but then he said in an amused tone:

"All women are like mosquitoes! Irritating, persistent! Very well, I will tell you where we are going, though I am quite certain that the information will tell you nothing and you will find little mention of such places in your guide-books."

"I hardly think I shall want one," Latonia said.

"Why should you say that?" he asked, which was what she had intended.

"Because the best guide, and of course the best one to give me information, would be you," she replied.

It was a satisfaction to see that even though he was aware that she had tricked him, there was quite a human twinkle in his eyes as he said:

"Very well, Latonia, you win. Now tell me exactly what you wish to know before we get there."

❋   ❋   ❋

The City they had reached, after travelling a great number of uncomfortable miles over uncharted roads and dusty plains, was like something out of another age.

Built of pale sandstone, the walls had a bleached appearance, as if the burning sun had drained them of colour. However, the bazaar was like a rainbow, but the people themselves looked poor and many were in rags.

For the best part of the journey Latonia had been able to ride, which was a joy she had not expected.

"I suppose you are used to riding long distances?" Lord Branscombe said to her before they reached the junction where they left the train.

"Yes, if you call a full day's hunting a long distance," Latonia replied.

She thought he should have been aware that Toni was as skilled in the saddle as her father had been.

Then as Lord Branscombe did not comment, she thought that because he disliked Toni and everything she stood for, he was not prepared for her to appreciate even the sports which he enjoyed.

She was glad, however, that she could ride as well as, if not better than, Toni and had been used to horses of more diverse quality than the well-trained, highly bred hunters which were always at her cousin's command.

The fine-boned horses that were waiting for her and Lord Branscombe were small and spirited, and Latonia realised when she first mounted hers that she would have to assert herself to keep it under control.

She was amused to see that Lord Branscombe's mount was also giving him a certain amount of trouble.

Finally the horses settled down, which gave Latonia a chance to inspect the countryside and to look at the people they passed by the wayside.

It was all a fascination and a joy she had not expected and she thought of thousands of questions she wanted to ask about the castes of the people they were passing, but she felt this was not the moment.

They had quite a caravan with them, including an elephant on which a lot of their luggage was piled and a whole army of servants who seemed to appear from nowhere, although she imagined some of them must have come on the train with them.

There were only two soldiers in uniform and she was not surprised that Lord Branscombe was also wearing his uniform of the Bengal Lancers.

She understood that this was a semi-official visit, but he still had the authority of the British Raj and his uniform was a symbol of it.

When he had worn it to arrive in Bombay, she had thought it made him look more distinguished and in a way more handsome than he had been when dressed as a civilian.

Now, riding a horse, she thought he was very impressive, and under any other circumstances it would have been exciting to be alone with such a good-looking man, in a world of their own.

"I am only his niece whom he dislikes," Latonia told herself, "and when he realises I have deceived him, he will undoubtedly hate me. Yet, if I had not come to India it would be something I would have regretted all my life."

She was thinking the same thing when their guides led them up the narrow streets of the City and there ahead of them was the Palace.

It was not a very impressive one, although Latonia was not aware of it, but she was to find later that it comprised half-a-dozen courtyards, a garden or two, and perhaps a hundred rooms.

The outer courtyards were filled with the Rajah's personal body-guards, who bowed low to Lord Branscombe as he rode by, pressing their palms and fingers together in the age-old greeting of the East.

Lord Branscombe and Latonia dismounted and were led by what was obviously a senior official into a large room which opened on to a garden.

It was very hot, and the crowds of privileged persons who sat cross-legged on the uncarpeted floor made it still hotter.

A shallow flight of steps led to a raised platform, and on this was a Throne where sat the Rajah in his robes of State, wearing ropes of pearls round his neck and a diamond-hilted sword.

He was a slim and impressive figure, except that for a young man he looked somewhat debauched and the pupils of his eyes were dilated. Latonia, looking at him with interest, was sure that he was addicted to opium.

He greeted Lord Branscombe with ceremony and he was bowed into a chair on the Rajah's side while Latonia was accommodated on a smaller chair beside him.

"We are deeply honoured by your presence, My Lord," the Rajah said in surprisingly good English.

Latonia learnt later that he had been educated at a British University.

"I am delighted to meet Your Highness," Lord Branscombe replied.

Latonia, listening intently, noted the geniality of his tone and the way, as the conversation continued, he complimented the young Prince and made it very obvious that he desired to be friendly.

Occasionally Latonia thought that his questions were searching, and she felt that some of the Indians in the room, especially those of high rank who were standing near the Rajah, were tense.

'They have something to hide,' she thought to herself, and wondered if Lord Branscombe was aware of it.

When their reception was over and they had accepted the sherbet which was offered them and eaten some of the sticky sweet-meats whose taste seemed to linger on the tongue long after they had been swallowed, Lord Branscombe and Latonia were taken to the Guest-House.

It was quite small and by no means as impressive

as the Palace, and Latonia saw with astonishment how shabby it was.

The paint was peeling from the walls, the covers and the furnishings were faded, and the table-cloth which covered the table at which they were to eat later in the evening was only rough-dried.

As if he sensed her surprise, as soon as they were alone Lord Branscombe explained:

"This is a poor State, but anyway you will find in India that although they paint the building when it is erected and when the Rajah takes a new bride, otherwise it remains untouched."

"How extraordinary!" Latonia exclaimed. "Personally I would rather have fewer diamonds on the hilt of my sword and more paint on the walls."

"You would never get His Highness to agree to that. His diamonds are very much a part of his prestige and actually they are not his but merely handed down from Rajah to Rajah and kept, except on ceremonial occasions like today, under lock and key."

"It is all fascinating," Latonia said. "Now, please tell me about His Highness."

Even as she spoke she realised that she had made a mistake, and Lord Branscombe replied in a slightly louder tone than he had used previously:

"We are indeed, my dear niece, very privileged to be guests of such a charming and intelligent young Ruler."

As he spoke, Lord Branscombe moved from the room in which they were talking on to the verandah so that he could look out at the garden which lay behind the Guest-House.

There was no sign of anyone, but Latonia, as she followed him, was quite certain that what he had said had been overheard and the information was at this very moment being carried to the Palace, where it would be related to the Rajah.

Chapter Five

Latonia did not get the chance to talk to Lord Branscombe alone for the next forty-eight hours.

She noticed that he was being charming and, for him, almost effusive to the young Rajah.

She thought that the young man responded, but she was aware that the pupils of His Highness's eyes were still dilated and she wondered if Lord Branscombe noticed it.

Addiction to opium was, as her father had told her, very prevalent in India, and she had learnt that English women were often afraid that their Ayahs would give the babies they looked after small amounts of opium to keep them quiet.

At the same time, the English allowed the sale of opium and, because it brought in much revenue in taxation, encouraged it.

Latonia found herself wondering if it was not something which could be stamped out by those who ruled the country, and she wished she could talk about such things to Lord Branscombe without his being suspicious of her motives in asking questions.

She found herself thinking how pleasant it would be if they could travel as ordinary people and she could learn from him so much about India, which she was beginning to find more fascinating every day.

In the afternoon of the second day of their visit they had watched a display of horsemanship and peg-sticking.

When the entertainment was over, Lord Branscombe and the Rajah walked away from his attendants ostensibly to inspect the Band. But Latonia was sure it was also to have a conversation which could not be overheard.

She felt that the older members of the Rajah's entourage were apprehensive about what was being said.

Their heads were all turned in the direction of the two men who were talking together, and they appeared to forget that they should in fact have been entertaining her because she had been left behind.

When the Rajah and Lord Branscombe came walking back towards them, she was sure that they heaved a sigh of relief.

The following morning when they said good-bye she thought that Lord Branscombe's speech of gratitude for the hospitality they had received was most eloquent.

Certainly their host seemed pleased, although she thought it might have been merely an expression of delight at their leaving.

Once again Latonia and Lord Branscombe were riding, while their attendants and the luggage followed at the more leisurely pace set by the sad-eyed bullocks who had to be prodded by their drivers to keep up even with the slow progress of the elephant.

They had left very early, so it was still comparatively cool, and when Lord Branscombe suggested that they should exercise their horses he and Latonia rode off on their own.

When finally they drew in their mounts to walk so that it was easy to converse, she said:

"Please tell me what you thought of the Rajah. Do you intend to recommend that his Province be given a British Resident?"

There was silence and she thought that Lord Branscombe intended either to refuse to answer or to snub her for her curiosity. But after a moment he said:

"As you are so interested, suppose you tell me what were your impressions."

Latonia glanced at him quickly. She had the feeling that he was testing her, perhaps trying to prove to his own satisfaction how stupid and frivolous she was.

She chose her words with care.

"I noticed as soon as we arrived that the Rajah was taking opium," she said. "I also thought that for such a young man he looked somewhat ... debauched."

She waited for Lord Branscombe to make some comment and after a distinct pause he asked:

"What else?"

"I may be wrong," Latonia answered, "but I felt that those in attendance on him, especially the older men, were tense and watchful. When you and the Rajah talked together yesterday afternoon, they were definitely apprehensive about what you were saying."

She stopped and saw that there was an undoubted look of surprise in Lord Branscombe's eyes.

"You are certainly very observant, Latonia."

"Am I right?" she questioned. "Did they have something to hide?"

As she spoke, she was thinking of Russian arms being supplied to the Rajah as they were to the tribesmen on the frontier, but she suspected that they were too far South for that to be a possibility.

"I did not expect to discuss such things with you," Lord Branscombe said, aware that she was waiting for his reply. "But perhaps I should make an exception."

"Please do," Latonia pleaded quickly, "and tell me what was wrong."

"Nothing very sensational," Lord Branscombe answered, "and it happens very often in these Princely States."

"What is that?"

"The Rajah, having had a European education, has new and progressive ideas, while his relatives are

determined to keep to the status-quo and make everything remain as it has been for the last thousand
years."

"Is that why they give him opium?"

"Exactly. Opium and women leave a young man
little time to concentrate on changes or to introduce
new policies."

"So you have decided that a British Resident
should be appointed?" Latonia ventured.

Lord Branscombe smiled.

"That may happen eventually, but I have given
His Highness a chance to prove himself."

"In what way?"

"I have told him that he has to cure his habit of
taking opium and must spend more time in the saddle,
inspecting his people, than in the women's quarters of
the palace."

"What did he say?" Latonia asked.

"He is intelligent when his brain is not fogged
with drugs, and because I flattered him quite a lot, he
was not offended when I told him that he must
behave like a man and assert himself."

"Do you think he will do so?"

"Quite frankly, I do not know the answer," Lord
Branscombe replied. "But I made it clear that if in six
months he has not changed his ways, I will recommend to the Viceroy that a British Resident be in-
stalled."

Latonia drew in her breath.

"Oh! I do hope he will listen to you."

"So do I," Lord Branscombe replied. "I hope, too,
that he survives."

Latonia's eyes were wide as she asked quickly:

"What do you mean by that?"

"There are many ways of disposing of young
Rajahs who try to break away from the traditions
which are considered sacred."

"What happens?"

"They die one way or another. There is a regrettable accident when they are out shooting; a fall; a snake-bite; something they eat which proves poisonous. Indians have used such methods since the beginning of time."

"You make it sound horrible and very dangerous," Latonia said in a low voice.

"Then forget it," Lord Branscombe answered sharply. "Perhaps things will be different at our next port-of-call."

This in fact was very much farther North, and they spent two nights in the train before they reached it.

Once again Latonia was fascinated by the crowds of sightseers and travellers at the stations and by the country through which they were passing.

She noticed the villages, which often consisted of just a little oasis of green standing, because of the lack of water, in what seemed little more than a desert. There would be a few shady trees, a central square with a well in the middle of it, and a pond for watering the cattle and the huge water-buffalo.

Latonia was also interested in the market-towns where, she learnt, the British had their Administrative Offices, shops, Police-Stations, hospitals, and of course Army Barracks.

It was all fascinating and she sat glued to the window until darkness fell with a swiftness that was almost like a curtain being dropped from the sky until the stars came out.

Although Lord Branscombe was most of the time immersed either in reading the newspapers or in writing what Latonia was sure was a report on the place they had just visited, he was at least prepared to talk while they had their meals.

These were brought onto the train at large stations and consisted of various dishes which tasted the same whatever they were called.

There was also dust which seemed to permeate everything, even with the windows and door closed.

At the same time, it was all new and exciting and an adventure.

Already she had discovered the atmosphere of India: the smell of spices and of wood-smoke, the blare of conches, the throbbing of distant tom-toms, and the muffled tread of bare feet on dusty ground.

She felt as if it had always been there like a half-forgotten dream in her mind or in her heart, only to rise now to reality like a phoenix from the ashes.

Sometimes, as if he could not resist the excitement in Latonia's shining eyes, Lord Branscombe would answer her questions without sounding cynical or suspicious of her reasons for asking them.

Outa, the next State they visited, was very beautiful.

There were lakes, shrines, and temples, scarlet-clad horsemen with fine moustaches and curved swords, and golden-skinned women walking like Queens as they carried brass *lotah*s on their proud heads.

Lord Branscombe and Latonia drove through a shfiting crowd who wore turbans and saris of vermilion, amber, turquoise, and green.

The Palace, set upon a ridge, was white with minarets, fretted windows, arches, and balconies. Through an immense triple gateway Latonia had a glimpse of a row of picketed elephants.

The Rajah, an old man with a white beard, had reigned for nearly thirty years. There was no doubt that he had his people well under control and the whole State revolved round him so that his slightest wish was law.

Latonia thought it would be impossible under these circumstances for Lord Branscombe to find anything wrong, but because by this time she had grown what she thought was almost a sixth sense where he was concerned, something told her that he was not satisfied.

They stayed three days and here she was allowed to go into the women's quarters, with its inner courtyards, its tank, and its sacred neem tree whose feathery leaves had medicinal virtues.

The Ranee was very young and pretty but unfortunately spoke only a few words of Urdu and no English.

Latonia tried to communicate with her and the other ladies by mime, but even when they showed her their jewels it was a somewhat laborious task and she felt relieved when the visit came to an end.

When they left, she and Lord Branscombe were provided with an open carriage drawn by two horses in which to drive to the nearest station.

"What did you think?" she asked eagerly as soon as they had finally waved to those who were seeing them off and to the crowds who threw flowers into the carriage as they passed.

"I am waiting to hear your assessment," Lord Branscombe replied.

"I thought everything seemed as it should be," Latonia answered, "but I knew you were suspicious."

"Did you think that was strange?"

"Not entirely, because ever since I have known you I have found you suspicious of something."

"Meaning yourself?"

"Yes."

"Well, perhaps the same applies both to you and to the State of Outa," he said. "You both appear to be too good to be true!"

"I am flattered," Latonia said. "But tell me, what did you discover?"

"Nothing," he answered. "I find that disconcerting, and, as you have already said, it makes me suspicious."

"Then what do you intend to do?"

"What can I do?" he asked. "But I have not yet heard the reports from those who stayed in Outa with us."

For a moment Latonia looked surprised, then she realised that she had been very silly.

Of course amongst the servants, many of them

being superior Indians, some were employed by Lord Branscombe to spy on his behalf on the people he was investigating.

It made her feel a little uncomfortable, and as if he knew what she was thinking Lord Branscombe said:

"Do I detect an air of condemnation about you?"

Latonia did not pretend not to understand.

"It seems somehow ... unsporting, or what in England we call ... not cricket," she replied.

Lord Branscombe laughed.

"There is one rule for England and another for India," he answered, "and I can assure you that the Rajah or any other host with whom we stay will expect those who accompany me to make investigations on my behalf, while taking every precaution to ensure that they find nothing incriminating."

"You make it sound like a game."

"That is exactly what it is," Lord Branscombe replied. "As the conquerors of India we have our ideas of what is right and just, while naturally the Indians do everything in their power to prevent our ideas superseding theirs, which they consider are better simply because they are steeped in tradition."

"But must you interfere?"

"We try not to, except when things are really wrong," Lord Branscombe explained, "such as the crimes committed by the thugs who kill thousands of people every year just because it is part of their religion; or the horrors of *Suttee*, and child-marriages in which many of the brides are no more than three to five years old!"

"I can understand that to insist on those reforms is right," Latonia said.

"And it is also right that our Empire should not be challenged by another power," Lord Branscombe said drily.

"Do you mean Russia?"

He nodded his head instead of speaking, and

Latonia thought that he did not wish to continue the conversation further.

She sat thinking over what he had said, until when they were once again in the train carrying them northwards she asked:

"Where are we going now?"

"Tonight, as it happens," Lord Branscombe replied, "we are staying in a Camp where a battalion of my Regiment is stationed."

Latonia looked interested as Lord Branscombe continued:

"I am afraid you will find it very dull, as I wish to dine in the Mess, where of course women are not permitted, and I understand that the Officers at this time of the year are not accompanied by their wives."

"What you are saying," Latonia replied, "is that I shall be left alone."

"Exactly," Lord Branscombe agreed, "although of course you will be properly guarded, with servants to wait on you and sentries outside the bungalow."

However, she thought that this was rather poor comfort when Lord Branscombe, looking resplendent in the evening-dress of the Bengal Lancers, left quite early in the evening to go to the Mess.

She was not impressed by the Barracks, which she was sure were typical of Regimental Barracks all over India.

There were rows of brick and plaster buildings for the English soldiers and huts for the Indian ones.

The ground on which they drilled was beaten-down sand without a hint of greenery or colour about it, and the children playing looked pale and emaciated from the heat and doubtless the wrong sort of food.

However, the bungalow in which Lord Branscombe and Latonia stayed was on the outskirts of the Camp and had a small garden which gave it a more attractive appearance.

There were the usual number of rooms and the inevitable verandah with wooden steps down to a straggling grass lawn.

The conventional furniture inside had, Latonia guessed, passed through the possession of numerous owners, losing some of its freshness every time it changed hands.

As they had been travelling since dawn, she was in fact quite glad that she did not have to make an effort at dinner-time to talk to Army Officers who would much rather be listening to Lord Branscombe.

At every station at which they stopped, there had always been Officers to greet him and spend the half-hour, or sometimes an hour, while the train waited, talking with him earnestly in low voices that prevented Latonia from hearing what they said.

"It is obviously a mission of importance and they are very impressed with him," she told herself.

She thought it was not surprising as he had such an air of distinction, and she could understand that his brother had resented his being so clever and rising so rapidly in the Army until he had, she thought, the aura of a hero about him.

Latonia could imagine him leading his troops into battle with his sword drawn, the men behind him prepared to follow him even if it meant they must die.

Then she told herself she was only being imaginative; doubtless Lord Branscombe would be the brains behind any encounter with an enemy but would leave the dash and the glory to younger men who only did what they were told to do.

When he had left and the sentries outside the bungalow had come sharply to attention as he climbed into the carriage which had been sent to collect him, Latonia sat down in the Sitting-Room and picked up a book.

As it was still very hot and she had been travelling all day, she felt sleepy and found it difficult to concentrate on what she was reading.

Dinner was ready for her a little later, but it was dull and unimaginative, consisting of the inevitable brown soup, a skinny chicken which had been alive earlier in the day, and a caramel pudding.

This apparently was the favourite dish of every *Memsahib* in India, and the servants who had learnt it from them found it easier to prepare than any other dish.

'I am sure that if I was allowed to do the house-keeping I would think of much more imaginative dishes,' Latonia thought.

She wondered if she dare suggest to Lord Branscombe that if they stayed for any length of time anywhere, she might choose the menus.

When dinner was over, she returned to the Sitting-Room, where an oil-lamp had been lit, and once again she took up her book.

Perhaps it was the slow-moving *punkah* overhead, or perhaps because her thoughts which turned into dreams were so much more interesting than what she was trying to read, she must have fallen asleep.

She awoke with a start to hear the sound of wheels, the jingle of horses' bridles, and the slap of the sentries' rifles as they came to attention.

'Lord Branscombe is back,' she thought.

She sat up quickly on the sofa, feeling glad that he had returned and she was no longer going to be alone.

She heard his footsteps cross the verandah and then he walked into the room, seeming to fill it with his presence, the light from the lamp glittering on the decorations on his chest.

Latonia was looking at his face and she thought he had a strange expression in his eyes to which, for the moment, she could not put a name.

"I thought you would not yet have retired to bed," he said, "so I have brought someone to meet you. Someone who I hope you will be pleased to see again."

As Latonia heard the last word of what Lord Branscombe was saying, she was intently on her guard! That he had said "again" made it obvious that she was to meet someone who knew Toni.

Then as she knew that what was about to happen constituted danger, a man came into the room.

She wondered frantically who he could be.

He was wearing the same uniform as Lord Branscombe, but he was not so tall and had, although he was young, a thin, lined face.

Desperately Latonia wondered what she should do and what she should say. She was well aware that Lord Branscombe was standing near her and looking at her in a manner that made her know he was watching for her reaction to the newcomer.

Then with a mocking note in his voice he said:

"Of course you will remember Andrew Luddington?"

Latonia drew in her breath and then as her eyes turned towards the visitor she saw his expression of bewilderment and surprise.

For a moment he did not speak, and then quite naturally he remarked:

"I am sorry, Sir, I must have misunderstood you. I thought you told me that your niece was staying with you."

It was Lord Branscombe's turn to look astonished.

"This *is* my niece," he replied.

There was a faint smile on Andrew Luddington's lips as he answered:

"That's as may be, Sir, but I was expecting to meet Latonia Combe, whom I knew in London. She was always called 'Toni.' Of course I might have guessed she would have no interest in coming to India when there is so much to keep her amused in England."

There was a tone of bitterness in his voice, and as if the disappointment of not finding whom he had hoped to see in the bungalow was unbearable, he said quickly:

100

"If you will excuse me, Sir, I will get back. It would be a mistake to keep the horses waiting."

It was quite obviously an excuse to get away, and as Andrew Luddington turned and started to walk back to the verandah from which he had come, Lord Branscombe followed him.

Latonia stood without moving until she heard the carriage drive away, and for one moment she felt that she must go too!

She wanted to run and hide even in the darkness of the garden rather than face Lord Branscombe.

Then a pride that she did not know she possessed made her stand where she was, her eyes seeming to fill her whole face as he came back into the room, closing the door behind him.

He walked towards her to stand looking at her so accusingly that she felt as if she were in the prisoners' dock.

"I suppose I am entitled to an explanation!"

"I am . . . sorry that I have . . . deceived you."

"If you are not my niece, then in the name of Heaven, who are you?"

"I . . . am . . . Latonia Hythe."

She saw a flicker of recognition in his eyes when she mentioned her name, and after a moment he asked:

"Do you mean that you are Arthur and Elizabeth Hythe's daughter?"

"Y-yes."

"I knew they had one because they talked about her, but perhaps you will inform me why you are here in the place of my niece, Latonia Combe?"

Latonia drew in her breath. Because of the sharp edge in Lord Branscombe's tone and the anger in his eyes, she felt as if her voice had died in her throat and it was impossible to speak.

"Toni . . . could not leave . . . England at this particular . . . moment," she faltered.

"What do you mean she *could* not?"

"She . . . she was in . . . love . . ."

It was difficult to say the words which seemed to come to her lips reluctantly.

"That is hardly anything new," Lord Branscombe said scathingly. "So, because of a fresh infatuation for another wretched man, whom she will doubtless treat in the same diabolical manner as she treated young Luddington, you and she thought up this incredible masquerade!"

"Toni is in . . . love as she has never been in . . . love before," Latonia said in a very small voice.

"If that was her excuse for not obeying my instructions, she might have had the courage and the decency to tell me so."

"Would you have . . . listened to her?"

Latonia felt as if she was being impertinent, and Lord Branscombe walked across the room before he said:

"I suppose I should have been suspicious when you turned out to be so different from what I expected. At the same time, I can hardly imagine a more disgraceful and underhanded deception than that you should take the place of my niece and put me in this position by your lies and deceit."

"I . . . I . . . am . . . sorry," Latonia said, "very . . . very . . . sorry."

"That is hardly enough!"

Lord Branscombe was silent and Latonia wondered frantically what else she could say. Then, as if he suddenly thought of it, he put his hand into the pocket of his tunic and said:

"Perhaps this will throw some light on your extraordinary behaviour. It was waiting for me when I reached the Mess, and because I thought that being a cable it might be bad news, I opened it."

He held it out to Latonia as he spoke, and she took it, aware that her fingers were trembling.

Because he was watching her she found it difficult for the moment to focus her eyes on what was

written. Then the words on the paper seemed to jump
out at her.

*We were married this morning. Ivan's father
died last week. Wildly happy. Love, T.*

Latonia gave a sigh of relief which seemed to
come from the very depth of her body.

"It is not... bad news," she said, "but very...
good news."

"I presume you are informing me, having read it,
that my niece is married," Lord Branscombe said.

"Yes, she is married, and as this says, as her
husband's father is dead... she is... now the Duchess of Hampton."

As she spoke, Latonia thought that if anything
could mitigate Lord Branscombe's anger, this should.
Since Toni was now a Duchess, no Guardian, however
difficult, could refuse to acknowledge that socially it
was a brilliant match.

She felt that there was a look of triumph in her
eyes as she went on:

"It would not matter to Toni whether Ivan was a
nobleman or a nobody. She loves him for himself, as
he loves her, and they will now, as they said before I
left, live happily ever after."

"It sounds delightful," Lord Branscombe said sar-
castically. "And I presume when you took part in this
diabolical plot to deceive me, it did not strike you that
you were putting your own hand into a hornet's
nest?"

Latonia did not understand, and as she looked at
him in a puzzled fashion, he said harshly:

"You cannot be so stupid as not to realise what
damage you have done to your reputation by travelling alone with me, pretending to be my niece when
you are in fact no relation."

The way he spoke was so scathing that almost
before she realised the full impact of what he was
saying, Latonia felt the blood rising in her cheeks.

"I . . . I . . . will go . . . home at . . . once," she said quickly, "and no-one will . . . know."

"Do you really believe that is possible?" Lord Branscombe asked. "The English papers will undoubtedly carry the announcement of my niece's marriage, especially as it is to someone of such social consequence as a Duke. There will naturally be people in India as in England who are aware that I do not have two nieces."

"I am of no consequence whatsoever," Latonia said. "My father and my mother, as you know, are dead, and except when Toni has been at the Castle, I have been living very quietly in the village with an old Governess to chaperone me."

She pleaded with him to understand as she continued:

"Toni has taken my place while I have been away, but even if anyone knew I had been to India it would not tell them very much. Why should they guess I have been with you?"

"I can only say," Lord Branscombe replied, "that I am astounded at your foolishness. I thought that you were intelligent."

It was as if he expected Latonia to speak, and when she did not do so, he went on:

"You did not meet anyone on the ship because I was determined that you should not do so, but you may be quite certain that a great number of passengers knew we were there and know who you were supposed to be."

Latonia made a little sound but he went on:

"Since we arrived you have met a large number of Officers who undoubtedly will tell their wives they have been introduced to you; and since they have little else to do, they have probably speculated with the other women as to why you are travelling with me."

Lord Branscombe's voice seemed to sharpen with every word he spoke and to become more accusing, more derogatory.

Latonia felt herself trembling, but she found it impossible not to go on looking at him, her eyes held by his.

It was almost as if he had deliberately forced her to be his prisoner while he berated her for her behaviour.

His reaction was exactly as she had suspected it would be when she was discovered. It was something which she had known was inevitable, but now that it was upon her she felt every nerve in her body shrink from him.

"There is ... nothing I can ... do except to ... disappear," she said in a very small voice. "Perhaps the people will ... forget about ... me. Perhaps ... you could say I was ... dead, like ... Papa and Mama."

When she mentioned them there was a little sob in her voice which was impossible for Lord Branscombe to miss.

Then he said, and she thought his voice was less harsh:

"There is, of course, one obvious solution, and if it does not meet your approval then you have no-one to blame but yourself."

"What ... is ... that?" Latonia asked.

"The only possible way in which I can save your reputation," he replied, "is to marry you!"

For a moment Latonia thought she could not have heard him correctly. She was sure she must be mistaken, and then as she drew in her breath he said angrily:

"There is nothing else I can do, and I can tell those who have already met you that we acted a part in order to conceal the fact that we were married indecently quickly after your parents' death."

His voice once again was sharply sarcastic as he went on:

"Doubtless you will be accused of being heartless and deceitful, but that is nothing to what would be said about you if the real truth came to light."

"But as I have already . . . said, I am of no . . . importance," Latonia said quickly, "so if I just . . . disappear it will not . . . really hurt . . . me."

"Can you really believe that?" Lord Branscombe asked. "My dear girl, you will be ostracised for life from every decent house in England and anywhere else in the world."

He paused before he went on:

"One whisper—and there would undoubtedly be more than one—that you have travelled for some weeks alone with a man, and then every respectable woman with whom you come into contact will sweep her skirts on one side as she passes you, in case she might be contaminated."

"What they . . . thought would . . . not be true," Latonia said childishly.

"You can hardly expect them to believe anything but the worst!" Lord Branscombe snapped. "And you must be aware that a woman who sins is never forgiven nor are her misdeeds ever forgotten."

"I . . . I . . . was only trying to . . . help . . . Toni," Latonia said. "She loves the . . . Marquis and his father wanted him to . . . marry a German Princess. She knew if she . . . went away with you, he might be . . . forced to do so."

"All I can say," Lord Branscombe replied, "is that he sounds the sort of weak young fool who is likely to be led by the nose by my disgracefully behaved niece!"

"You are twisting . . . everything and making it . . . sound horrible," Latonia cried. "The Marquis adores Toni, he does really! I saw them together and there was no question of any . . . pretence. She loves him as she has never loved any man in her whole life."

She drew in her breath as if to give herself courage before she added:

"I know you will not . . . believe this, because you are so . . . angry with Toni and have said such . . . horrible things to me when you thought I was she. But it is really not her . . . fault that men fall in love with her because she is so lovely and . . . attractive."

She paused, as if thinking back, before she went on:

"It has been the same ever since she was a very young girl. There is something . . . irresistible about her."

"Do you think that justifies her behaviour or excuses her in making use of you?"

"I have already told you that I do not matter," Latonia replied. "I have always lived a very quiet life because we never had any money. Toni was even more than a sister to me . . . more like a . . . twin! Whatever I have done, I have done it gladly for her and I am prepared to suffer the consequences without . . . complaint."

The sincerity in her voice seemed to ring out in the small room.

"But that does not release me from my obligations," Lord Branscombe said after a moment's silence. "I suppose . . . in a way it is my fault that I did not come to the Castle to collect my niece, in which case none of this would have happened."

"Do not blame yourself," Latonia replied quickly. "I expect since Toni was so . . . determined to stay with the Marquis that she would have found some other way not to come with you to . . . India."

As she spoke, she thought Lord Branscombe's lips tightened, and she added:

"I know it is difficult for you, but please try to understand. Toni is not bad, as you think. She is impulsive, sometimes unpredictable, because she enjoys life so much and it was terribly dull for her living at the Castle."

She saw the surprise in Lord Branscombe's eyes and she went on:

"Once when we were going home to our own small house, leaving Toni behind at the Castle, Mama said that she was so very sorry for the lonely little girl who could not come with us."

"I should have thought that with my brother's position and his enormous wealth, my niece could have had anything in life that she desired."

"Except . . . love," Latonia said softly. "That is what she lacked . . . love and people round her who loved each other as Mama loved Papa and he loved her."

She thought she had made him think, and she went on before he could speak:

"You saw Mama and Papa together . . . they were with you before they died, and you must have realised how happy they were. It was not money that counted in our home, it was the happiness which came from . . . love, and that is . . . something Toni . . . never had."

There were tears in Latonia's eyes as she spoke, firstly because she wanted so much to make him understand the reason for Toni's behaviour and secondly because her father and mother had died so recently that it was impossible for her to speak about them without wanting to burst into tears.

Now her eyes were misty and she turned away from Lord Branscombe and moved deliberately towards the door.

When she reached it she stopped for a moment to say:

"I am . . . sorry, I can only . . . apologise abjectly for . . . everything I have done . . . for every lie I have . . . told you. I know Mama would be . . . shocked at my . . . deceiving you, but there was no other way in which Toni could be . . . with the . . . Marquis. Perhaps when you . . . think it . . . over you will be able to . . . forgive her and . . . me."

As Latonia finished speaking the tears overflowed and ran down her cheeks.

Because she did not want Lord Branscombe to see them, she went quickly from the room to hide herself in her own bedroom.

Chapter Six

Because she had cried for a long time after going to bed, Latonia felt she had only just fallen asleep when she heard somebody knocking on the door.

"What is it?" she asked.

"Lord Sahib leave in one hour, *Memsahib*," the servant replied.

"I will be ready," Latonia managed to answer.

She got up and dressed hurriedly, but by the time she reached the verandah, where she knew breakfast would be served, it was to find that Lord Branscombe had already left.

She thought he would be having breakfast with some of his brother-Officers, and she was glad she did not have to face him after the storm of yesterday evening.

She might have known, she thought, that sooner or later somebody from Toni's past would confront her.

However, she had not expected it would be Andrew Luddington, because she had not realised that he was with the Bengal Lancers.

She could understand now why Lord Branscombe was so infuriated with Toni for driving him to attempt suicide, not only because he was an impressionable young man but also because he was in his own Regiment.

"Whatever His Lordship may think," Latonia told herself, "I still consider that Andrew Luddington is weak and lacking in self-control to have behaved as he did."

She knew it would be no use saying so, as she waited for Lord Branscombe to return, anticipating that he would start his condemnation of Toni's conduct all over again, besides the fact that he was appalled by the deception which both she and her cousin had practised on him.

She could not believe that he was speaking seriously when he had said that the only solution for the consequences of her deceitful behaviour was to accept his offer of marriage.

'He was just threatening me and trying to make me nervous and apprehensive,' Latonia thought.

At the same time, it struck her that if or when the deception became known, she would not be the only one to suffer.

It would appear very reprehensible of Lord Branscombe that on his visits as a representative of the Viceroy he should take a young woman with him, introducing her as a relative when she actually was nothing of the sort.

'I must go home ... I must leave India ... immediately!' Latonia thought in a sudden panic.

She decided she would tell Lord Branscombe the moment he returned.

It was fortunate that she had the money for her fare, but she was aware that she had no idea how to get back to Bombay from where she was at this moment, and she also knew it would be impossible for her to make the journey alone.

Every minute she waited for Lord Branscombe seemed to make the difficulties worse than they were already.

When finally he appeared, there was however no chance for her to speak with him alone.

He came back with two senior Officers, and there was already a carriage waiting to carry them to the railway-station which was only a mile or so from the Camp.

There was no time for Latonia to do anything but pick up her sunshade, her bag, and her gloves, and step into the carriage to drive off with Lord Branscombe beside her and the two Officers seated opposite them.

When they reached the station there were the usual large number of servants to attend to their needs, and their own special carriage had already been attached to the morning train heading North.

Latonia thought that Lord Branscombe gave the order for the train to move sooner than was usual.

It amused her that at all the stations at which they had stopped the guard always asked Lord Branscombe's permission before he signalled the engine-driver to start the train.

Now the Officers quickly said good-bye, and once again Latonia and Lord Branscombe were alone in their Drawing-Room.

Latonia glanced at him apprehensively.

She thought he looked grim and there was a tightness about his lips, but he merely handed her one of the newspapers that had been put out for them and she saw that it was a three-weeks-old *Times* from England.

As she realised that he did not wish to talk, she opened it, although she found it hard to concentrate on the political difficulties at home and on the description of the Foreign Royalty being entertained by the Queen at Windsor.

It was nearly three-quarters-of-an-hour before the train slowed down and stopped at what Latonia saw with surprise was a very small station.

She had grown used to the huge crowds, but now instead there were only two or three people on the platform who were looking at the train in astonishment.

Beyond the station she could see in the distance a small village and from there a number of people, mostly children, were running excitedly towards them.

It struck her that they had not expected the train to stop, and for the first time since they had left the Camp she spoke to Lord Branscombe.

"Why are we stopping here?" she asked.

"I will tell you why in a few minutes," he replied.

She was surprised, but she did not like to question him further, as a servant had come into the compartment with glasses of fruit-juice and slices of papaya.

Latonia sipped the juice, wondering what was happening, but Lord Branscombe continued to be absorbed in the newspapers and she did not ask any further questions.

When they had waited at the small station for nearly twenty minutes, one of the senior servants who was travelling with them came into the Drawing-Room.

He approached Lord Branscombe to say in a low voice:

"Everything arranged, Lord Sahib."

Lord Branscombe rose to his feet, saying:

"Come with me, Latonia!"

There was something in the way he spoke which made her feel frightened.

They stepped out of the train onto the platform and she saw waiting outside a rough cart quite different from anything she had travelled in before.

It was drawn by a young horse, and when she and Lord Branscombe had got into it and were seated on the hard seats, they set off at quite a good pace.

They were followed by a large number of small children running along the dusty road beside the cart, shouting at them and holding up their hands, asking for *baksheesh*.

This prevented Latonia from asking questions. She also had the uncomfortable feeling that Lord Branscombe had no intention of telling her what she wanted to know.

Because the horse was moving quickly they grad-

ually left the children behind and now on the outskirts of the village she saw a small building with a tin
roof, which, before she even saw the cross over the
door, she knew to be a Church.

It was only as the horse slowed down that Latonia
turned her face towards Lord Branscombe to say
frantically:

"P-please . . . we must not . . . do this! It is . . .
wrong!"

"It is the only thing we can do," he replied
firmly.

She wanted to protest, she wanted to plead with
him, but at that moment the horse came to a standstill
and a man appeared at the door of the Church.

He was tall and gaunt, wearing a black cassock.
Latonia thought he must be a Missionary.

Lord Branscombe stepped out of the cart and
shook him by the hand, and as he did so the Parson
said:

"I understand from your servant, Mr. Combe,
that you wish to be married."

"That is correct," Lord Branscombe answered,
"and this is my future wife, Miss Hythe."

The Parson shook hands with Latonia, then
walked ahead of them into the Church.

It was very primitive, and Latonia thought, from
the bareness of the walls and the lack of flowers and
candles, that it was Presbyterian.

As if he had been told that speed was essential,
the Parson picked up a Prayer-Book, then as Latonia
and Lord Branscombe stood before him, he began the
Marriage Service.

❋   ❋   ❋

For the rest of the day as the train continued on
its way North, Latonia felt as if she were existing in a
dream.

She could not believe that she had actually been
married, and it had been done in such a strange and
austere manner that it was impossible to feel that she

113

was a bride or that Lord Branscombe was her husband.

The only reality was his plain gold signet-ring on the third finger of her left hand, which because he had worn it on his little finger was only slightly too large for her. But it seemed like a heavy chain that made her a prisoner for all time.

How could she really be married?

How could she be the wife of a man who despised and hated her and who had been forced into matrimony because she and Toni had deceived him?

"What can I say? What can I do?" Latonia asked herself despairingly, but she could find no answer.

They did not reach their destination until late in the afternoon, when it was not so hot.

Latonia wanted to ask where they were going but she was too afraid to speak, and she had only been able to stare out the window at the limitless plains through which they were passing, which seemed symbolic of the emptiness of her own future.

Then, before she had expected it, they arrived at their destination and were riding through a City where she saw the familiar sights of the heaped colours of fruit, vegetables, and grain in the bazaar and the teeming, jostling crowds amongst whom moved the great lazy Brahmin bulls sacred to Shiva.

She had a glimpse of stalls which sold glass bangles and brilliant saris of red, blue, gold, and grass green.

Then they were through the City and once again there was a Palace with gleaming turrets and latticed windows sadly in need of paint.

There were the inevitable attendants welcoming them and a Reception in the huge Throne-Room.

This time the Rajah, who appeared to be middle-aged, seemed to Latonia to be less pleasant than their previous hosts had been.

It was not that he was impolite, it was just that

she felt he exuded something that made her feel he was cruel and perhaps wicked.

It was only an impression, and she wondered if Lord Branscombe felt the same way about him.

But, as she had learnt to expect, he was extremely affable, greeting the Rajah on behalf of the Viceroy and paying him the compliments that were always expected in the East.

Now for the first time Latonia was presented by Lord Branscombe as his wife.

"I did not know you were married, My Lord," the Rajah said in quite intelligible English.

"I have only just returned from England," Lord Branscombe explained, "and few people are yet aware that my wife is travelling with me."

"I am honoured to be one of Her Ladyship's first hosts," the Rajah said, "and of course we must celebrate such a happy event. I am sure Lady Branscombe will enjoy our dancers."

"It will be a privilege for us both to see them," Lord Branscombe replied before Latonia could speak.

The Guest-House was very much the same as the other Guest-Houses had been, and there were a large number of servants to wait on them who Latonia was sure by now included one who could understand their conversation and report it to the Palace.

Tonight, as their host was Muslim, they could dine with him, whereas the previous Rajah had been Hindu, which meant they ate alone.

Latonia put on one of her prettiest gowns, feeling that although Lord Branscombe might dislike her, as his wife she must at least try to do him credit.

She thought that as a married woman she might be expected to wear jewellery, but her neck was bare and her only ornamentation was the glitter of the gold ring on her finger.

Because she was nervous she took not only more trouble but also more time than usual over arrranging her hair.

When finally she went from her bedroom into the Sitting-Room it was to find Lord Branscombe standing waiting for her in a manner which told her without words that she was late.

"I am ... sorry ..." she began, but he moved impatiently towards the door and she could only follow him outside to step into a carriage that was waiting for them.

They drove in silence the short distance to the Palace.

Although it only took a few minutes, Latonia found herself wondering how she could bear a lifetime of feeling that her husband was as unapproachable as the snowy peaks of the Himalayas.

They were received at the Palace with the ceremony with which Latonia was now familiar.

The Rajah, even more resplendent than he had been earlier in the day, was glittering with jewels, but, as before, Latonia felt there was an evil glint not only in his eyes but in his emeralds, while the rubies that he wore in his turban seemed to burn with an ill-omened fire.

"I am just being imaginative," she told herself.

Yet, as she had known at the first Palace they had visited, there was an indisputable feeling of animosity from the elderly courtiers in attendance.

While their lips smiled, their eyes were wary and suspicious.

"There is something wrong here ... something very wrong!" Latonia told herself.

She longed to know if Lord Branscombe felt the same, but he was talking easily and pleasantly with the Rajah and there was nothing in his quiet, controlled voice to frighten anyone.

Because she was tired and beset by her own problems she found it difficult to concentrate on the dancing or to try to understand the story which the women portrayed with their movements.

All that the music seemed to be telling her was that she was married, and while Toni could cable she was "wildly happy" those were words which Latonia would never be able to say.

It seemed impossible to think that it had really happened, and yet it had, and her dream of falling in love and finding a man who would love her as her father had loved her mother was lying broken in pieces at her feet.

"How could I have been so foolish as not to realise that this might occur?" Latonia asked herself.

But she knew that never in her wildest dreams had she imagined that the end of the masquerade which Toni had thought up for her would be marriage.

She had expected Lord Branscombe to be angry; she had anticipated that she might be sent home in disgrace; but it had never crossed her mind that instead he would make her his wife because it was the only way they could avoid an unpleasant scandal which would harm them both.

Now Latonia could see only too clearly how stupid she had been.

India then had seemed far away and she had merely thought that when she returned to England, anything that had happened in that far-off Continent would be forgotten.

Instead she should have worked out in her own mind that Lord Branscombe was far too important a man not to be watched, gossipped about, and, not unnaturally, envied.

She told herself reluctantly that, horrifying though it might seem to her, he had done the only thing possible in the circumstances in which he found himself.

He had been very clever about it too.

She was sure that the Missionary in the small village where they had been married was not likely to read either the newspapers from England or those that were published in India.

She had felt that he was a man dedicated to the

117

conversion of souls and that the Social World was something that would never encroach upon his mind because it would not be of the least interest to him.

To him, Kenrick Combe was just an ordinary Englishman, and he was unlikely to connect him in any way with the pomp and grandeur of the British Raj.

'Lord Branscombe has been clever,' Latonia thought, 'while I have been half-witted and deserve the punishment that has been meted out to me.'

Her feeling of humility lasted throughout the evening, and as they drove back to the Guest-House she wondered if she should tell Lord Branscombe how sorry she was.

But when they stepped into the Sitting-Room there was a servant to ask if there was anything they required, and before he could leave the room Lord Branscombe said abruptly:

"Good-night, Latonia! I hope you sleep well."

As he spoke he walked towards his own bedroom. Latonia realised that they were next door to each other but she thought that as far as their minds and hearts were concerned, they might as well be a world apart.

As she undressed she saw that their bedrooms communicated.

There was a door which she had not noticed when she was dressing because it was covered by a curtain of glass beads.

Beyond it she could faintly hear Lord Branscombe moving about.

She sat down at the dressing-table and, looking at herself in the mirror, wondered what her mother would say if she knew that this was her wedding-night and she was spending it not only alone but in disgrace.

Her mother had often spoken of how happy she had been on her honeymoon.

"Your father was the most handsome, attractive man I had ever seen in my life," she had said to

Latonia once, "and when I was married to him, I felt as if we were in Paradise together and there was no-one else in the whole universe except ourselves."

"That is what I want to feel," Latonia told her reflection, and she knew that entirely through her own stupidity it was lost to her forever.

When she was in bed she found it impossible to sleep but lay listening to the soft sounds outside her bedroom window.

She thought she recognised the creak of a well-wheel, the distant bark of a pariah dog, a baby crying, and an old man, perhaps a night-watchman, clearing his throat.

The sounds were mingled and mixed with the scent of orange-blossom and jasmine and the smell of warm dust and sun-baked stones.

'If I loved somebody,' Latonia thought, 'India would be a perfect background for our love.'

Two hours later she was still awake and was tossing and turning on her bed because she felt hot and sticky.

She thought she would go to wash in the bathroom which was connected to her bedroom. Although the water might be tepid instead of cold, at least she would feel more comfortable.

She got out of bed and pushed open the door, and as she did so she heard a voice speaking in a whisper.

It was an eerie sound which held something of a faint, hollow echo.

For a moment she stood very still, with her hand on the door, shivering and feeling a little frightened.

Then she realised that the voice was speaking in Urdu and the ghostly echo was accounted for by the fact that there was a wide stone sluice-pipe which carried off the water from the bath.

She had heard the sound before, at the first Guest-House in which they stayed, and she had been startled by it although then it had been daylight.

Now she realised that somebody was talking on

the far side of the bathroom wall, unaware that the
sluice was acting as a kind of speaking-tube.

The voice continued, and now Latonia picked out
some words she could understand.

"He will—die!"

"Is that wise?" another voice asked.

"It is—necessary. If the Lord Sahib find what
we—hide there will be trouble—big trouble!"

"Big trouble if Lord Sahib die!"

"No, *datura* not like gun or knife. Give *datura* at
breakfast to Lord Sahib, then he die in train."

"Good idea!"

Latonia drew in her breath; then, very softly,
moving one foot behind the other, she retreated from
the bathroom back into the bedroom.

Now as the full horror of what she had heard
swept over her, she remembered what *datura* was and
how they intended to kill Lord Branscombe.

She had read about it in several of the books that
she had studied while coming over in the ship and
had learnt that it was a plant that grew wild in many
parts of India and had lily-like flowers that were
sweetly scented and very beautiful. But the seeds,
which were brown and green, were known as the
"apples of death."

Very poisonous, it had, Latonia read, been used
for centuries as a handy method of disposing of
unwanted husbands, surplus wives, and elderly relatives.

One book which had been most specific on its use
had told her that it was the commonest of all poisons
and when ground into a powder and mixed with food,
bread being the usual choice, it was fatal.

And death, Latonia remembered now, depended
entirely on the manner in which *datura* had been
eaten. Swallowed quickly, even a little bit was fatally
effective.

She told herself that she must warn Lord Branscombe at once, but as she moved quickly towards the

door which communicated between their rooms, she thought of something else.

It was a soft movement which alerted her; a movement so slight that, had she not been awake and standing up, she might not have heard it.

But she knew exactly what it was, and that servants, doubtless on the instructions of the Rajah, were sleeping outside their rooms.

It was customary in India for a distinguished guest to be protected in such a manner, but now Latonia realised how vulnerable they were and how difficult it would be to warn Lord Branscombe of what was happening when anything they said could be overheard.

There was a wide verandah outside their bedrooms and there would doubtless be servants sleeping out there too. But they would not be able to hear so well as those inside, who had their ears against the doors, which, warped with the heat, did not fit closely.

She stood, irresolute, feeling for a moment as if she was besieged on all sides by an enemy who had coiled himself round them like a snake.

She could of course wait for the morning, then suggest to Lord Branscombe that before they ate breakfast they should walk in the garden and admire the flowers.

There they would be able to talk without it reaching the ears of those who would listen.

"But suppose," she reasoned to herself, "the poisoners strike before breakfast?"

The English habit of being called with tea and several thin pieces of bread and butter had been introduced into India by the Sahibs and their wives.

Here in the Guest-House, an unsuspected piece of bread and butter could easily kill Lord Branscombe before she could warn him.

'I have to tell him now ... now at this moment!' Latonia thought.

121

She knew it would be impossible for her to sleep until she had told him what she had overheard.

Resolutely, because she was feeling both afraid and shy, she walked towards the door that was covered by the bead curtain and, putting her hand through it, found the handle.

For one terrifying moment she thought that perhaps the door was locked, but then it opened and she walked into Lord Branscombe's room.

It was larger than hers, and by the faint light that shone through the uncurtained window, which came from a light that remained burning all night on the verandah, she could see the outline of the bed.

The mosquito-curtaining heaped high above it had not been lowered as they were so far North.

Latonia stood where she was, trying to see where she was going and to think of what she should say.

Then she tiptoed towards the bed, her bare feet making no sound on the native woven mats which covered the wooden floor. She had actually reached Lord Branscombe's side when, with the alertness of a man used to danger, he awoke.

He moved, and although Latonia could not see clearly, she knew his eyes were open and he was aware of her standing beside him, silhouetted against the faint light from the window.

"What is it? Who are you?" he asked.

Then, with what was undoubtedly an incredulous note in his voice, he exclaimed:

"Latonia!"

There was no doubt now, Latonia thought, that the servant outside would be listening, and she said quickly and loudly enough for him to overhear easily:

"You . . . forgot to . . . come and say . . . good-night to me as I . . . expected you . . . to."

Because she knew that he must be staring at her incredulously, she added quickly:

"I . . . I fell asleep . . . or I would have . . . come to you before."

Lord Branscombe did not speak and Latonia thought despairingly that she would never make him understand.

Then, because she knew that if she failed he would die, it was almost as if a voice told her what she must do.

Without thinking, without even considering anything but the horror of what she had overheard, she moved forward and lay down on the bed beside Lord Branscombe.

As she did so, she was aware that he stiffened, but the only thing that mattered was that he should know there were plans to kill him.

In the swiftness of a second Latonia was beside him, her head was on the pillow, and her lips were close to his ear.

"I have ... something to tell ... you," she whispered.

Her voice was so low that she could barely hear it herself, but as if at last he understood he said aloud:

"I am glad you came to me. I thought you would be asleep. It has been a long day."

As he finished speaking, Latonia whispered:

"There is ... danger! They ... intend to ... kill you!"

"How do you know this?"

His voice was as low as hers.

"I overheard, through the sluice-pipe, two men talking," she whispered.

Again speaking aloud, Lord Branscombe said:

"You must not overtire yourself. I was afraid the party tonight on top of the long journey would be too much for you."

"I am all right."

"How do they intend to kill me?" he whispered.

"With *datura*," Latonia replied. "Either at breakfast, or it might be in something you eat earlier. Please ... be careful!"

"I will be," he murmured; then aloud:

"There will be another long journey tomorrow, so I think you should go back to your own bed, and I hope I do not wake you when I get up early."

"I expect I will sleep soundly."

Latonia lowered her voice as she said:

"Suppose they ... try another ... method? Please ... please stay here until we ... leave."

Her voice rose a little because she was agitated. Then as if she remembered the servants outside, she added in a whisper:

"There is ... somebody ... listening outside the ... door."

"I know," Lord Branscombe replied, "and so we might as well give them something to listen to!"

As he spoke he raised his head, then his mouth came down on hers.

For a moment Latonia was too astonished to feel anything but surprise.

All she felt at first was the hardness of his lips. Then his kiss seemed to soften and become more compelling and at the same time more demanding.

She had never been kissed before, and yet strangely enough it was exactly how she thought a kiss would be: a feeling of being captured and conquered.

Then his lips gave her a strange warmth that seemed to tingle through her body and become almost a river of flame moving upwards through her breasts, through her throat, and into her lips.

It was so wonderful, so different from any emotion she had ever felt before, that she felt her whole being respond to it, and as she did so she knew that this was what she had been seeking, what she had been longing for.

This was love, and she had not realised it.

Love for a man of whom she had been vividly conscious for the last days and weeks, and who had filled her mind, whether she was aware of it or not, from the first thing in the morning until the last thing at night.

Her fear of him, or what had at first been a hatred, had changed, without her knowing it, to love; the love which now made her feel as if he carried her away into the starlit darkness outside and they were no longer human.

Even as she wanted him to go on kissing her more than she had ever wanted anything in her whole life, she was free and he said in a strange voice:

"Go back to bed, Latonia. It is too late for love-making tonight. But I am glad that you came to me."

As he spoke, Lord Branscombe put his head back on the pillow and turned his back towards her.

She was dismissed, and Latonia felt as if she fell from the very highest peak of a mountain down into the darkness of the valley beneath.

For a moment it was impossible to move, impossible to adjust herself to reality.

She had touched the Divine, but, she thought despairingly, it had only been play-acting on his part, for the servants who were listening outside the door.

Slowly, feeling as if for the moment her limbs would not obey her, she slipped off the bed.

As her feet touched the ground, she wanted once again to beg Lord Branscombe to be careful.

How could he die now when he had taught her what really being alive was like?

Then, with a throb of her heart which was like the stab of a dagger, she realised that he did not feel for her what she felt for him.

They were back exactly where they had been before. He was hating and despising her, and the wonder he had given her with his lips had meant nothing to him.

Slowly, because suddenly she felt that she was moving in a nightmare, Latonia walked across the room.

Only as she reached the door did she look back.

It was impossible to distinguish clearly in the darkness, but she thought that Lord Branscombe was lying as she had just left him, with his back to where she had been, his head turned sideways, and he was not even watching her go.

"Good-night," she murmured.

He did not answer and she went through the bead curtain and heard it jingle into place behind her.

* * *

In bed again, Latonia lay for a long time looking at the door which now divided her from the man whose name she bore.

She knew now that what she wanted to do was go back, lie beside him, and ask him to kiss her again.

It would be an outrageously immodest thing for her to do, and yet because the servant was listening he would not be able to refuse her.

She felt as if a voice was tempting her to do just that, telling her that this might be the last chance, and once they were alone again they would sit in silence as they had after they were married.

She had felt then as if Lord Branscombe could not bear to look at her and she thought that he had been feeling not only angry but appalled that he had been tricked into having as his wife the last woman on earth he would have chosen for such a position.

"The last woman but one!" Latonia corrected herself wryly, for she was certain that Toni was even lower in his estimation than she was herself.

And yet there was little to choose between them!

They had both behaved in an outrageous manner, they had both been irresponsible to the point where their plot had resulted in unforeseen repercussions to which there appeared to be no ending.

'But only for me!' Latonia thought. Toni was safe. Toni was married to the man she loved. Toni . . .

Latonia stopped suddenly.

She too was married to the man she loved. The only difference was that he did not love her.

How could she have guessed, how could she even for a moment have anticipated that she would fall in love with Lord Branscombe despite his feelings for her?

His lips had not only made her aware of her love for him but had brought her a rapture that was beyond anything she had ever imagined.

She shut her eyes to feel again that strange warmth rising through her body until it became a flame.

"No wonder," she told herself, "that the Indians worship the God of Love and sing songs in homage to him."

Love for them was part of their very lives, but Latonia was sure that to Lord Branscombe it was something that was of little importance.

"I love him!" she whispered into the darkness, and wondered what she could do about it.

How could she ever make him love her in return? How could she evoke in him the rapture and wonder he had given her?

Last night in bed she had cried bitterly and despairingly and she had thought it was because, having discovered her deception, he was angry with her.

But now she knew it was much more than that. It was because she wanted him to admire her, to trust her, and most of all, although she had not been aware of it, to love her.

He had always seemed so magnificent, especially in his uniform. But it was not only his looks which drew her and held her, but the aura of power and authority that he exuded, and something else . . . something which she knew was in every way the opposite of what she had felt coming from the Rajah's Palace.

It was in fact an aura of all that was honourable, good, and upright. Perhaps "noble" was the right word.

She thought in despair that because he was all

these things, in contrast it only made her deception seem worse.

"He will never love me," Latonia told herself. "He will only despise me for the rest of our lives together."

Then once again the tears came, tears that were a torture because she was crying for something she had never had—his love.

Chapter Seven

Latonia could not sleep and lay awake going over and over the same unhappy thoughts.

Then as the dawn came swiftly, the sun lighting first the ceiling of her room and then flooding everything with a golden light, she heard voices next door and knew that Lord Branscombe was rising.

His movements made her long to cry out in agony that he was taking an unnecessary risk.

How could he be so foolish, after what she had told him, as to go out into the danger that was lurking outside?

The men she had overheard talking had said he was to be poisoned, but perhaps by now the Rajah and those who were intriguing with him had thought of some other way in which he could meet his death.

She felt despairingly that anything she did would only strengthen Lord Branscombe's determination to behave normally and to keep whatever appointment it was he had made and above all to show no fear.

She heard him walking about in the next room, then as she lay tense and heard his footsteps walking down the passage she knew that there was nothing now for her to do but wait.

Because she was so afraid, she almost expected to hear a shot ring out or the cry of a man who had been knifed, but there were only the songs of the birds outside and all the usual sounds of a world waking to a new day.

Now there were the distant noises of high, female voices, of children laughing, and somewhere far in the distance, but nevertheless distinctive, the clatter of cooking-pots.

The sounds seemed all the more menacing because they were ordinary and familiar, and yet somewhere in the midst of them was a man whose enemies had doomed him to die.

For the moment there was nothing she could do but pray—pray as she had never prayed before in her life—for his safety.

"Please, God ... please ..."

She felt as if her prayers were turning round and round on a small wheel and there was no beginning or end to them, merely an eternal plea for help and for mercy.

She must have prayed for nearly an hour when she remembered that Lord Branscombe had said they were leaving today.

She rose, and when she was washing in the bathroom she heard somebody come into her room to call her.

She knew that when she returned she would find a pot of tea on a tray beside her bed, and she wondered if that too was poisoned, or if they would take the chance of her eating the same food at breakfast as Lord Branscombe.

Then she remembered that as she was only a woman, an inferior creature in Indian eyes, it would not be of any importance to them whether she lived or died.

Their target was Lord Branscombe and every weapon would be directed against him.

She washed quickly, thinking as she looked at the water-sluice how fortunate it was that she had heard the voices through it.

At least for the time being it had saved Lord Branscombe, but at the thought that he might have ridden determinedly into danger, she ran to the bedroom and dressed herself quicker than she had ever dressed before in her life.

She had decided to wait in her own room until she had heard him return, but when she was ready she found it impossible to do so.

She walked in a carefully controlled manner, because she actually longed to run, along the passage which led to the verandah.

As she had expected, breakfast was laid outside on a part of the verandah which overlooked the garden.

Because she had seen so often the carefully laid table with its unironed tablecloth and its silver which needed cleaning, she thought for a moment that perhaps she had imagined the whole thing.

How could there really be a dangerous, life-destroying poison waiting in what seemed so harmless and ordinary a meal?

Then she saw one of the servants in his colourful turban and clean white *dhoti* come from the house, carrying in his hand a small native woven basket in which was laid the newly baked *chipattis*—the unleavened bread which was always served in India.

He set the basket down on the table and as he did so Latonia knew with an instinct which could not be denied that the *chipattis* were poisoned and that the servant who placed them there was aware of it.

She clenched her hands together to control herself from crying out at the perfidy of it.

Lord Branscombe was a guest of the Rajah and it was, she knew, against every law of Eastern hospitality that he should be murdered by the host he trusted.

She walked to the front of the verandah and held on to the railings to look out over the garden with its colorful flowers and a lawn which, despite frequent watering, was green only in patches.

The trees were brilliant with blossoms and, silhouetted against the blue of the sky, they were a picture of beauty.

But Latonia could see nothing except the darkness, the treachery, and the evil which she had felt from the moment she had entered the Rajah's Palace.

A voice beside her made her start.

"Lady *Memsahib* wait for Lord Sahib?" a servant enquired.

It took her a second to concentrate on what the man was saying, then she longed to reply that she had no wish to die any sooner than was necessary.

But she knew that if she said anything which would put those who wished to kill Lord Branscombe on their guard, they would undoubtedly find another way of destroying him.

Instead she shook her head and replied in a voice which sounded deceptively calm:

"Yes, I will wait for the Lord Sahib."

With a bow the servant withdrew.

Latonia waited and went on waiting. It did not seem possible that time could pass so slowly.

Then just as she was beginning to grow frantic in case her worst fears were realised and Lord Branscombe had already met with a "regrettable accident" or had disappeared completely, he came walking down the passage from the front of the house and out onto the verandah.

She was so relieved to see him that she turned and made a little sound that was almost a cry of joy.

"I am sorry if I have kept you waiting," he said in such an ordinary tone that it swept away the questions which hovered on her lips.

He walked towards the breakfast-table, remarking:

"You should not have waited for me."

Because Latonia knew that she must play the part that was expected of her, she moved towards him and said the first thing that came into her head:

"I was ... watching the ... birds."

She only realised it now, but there were as usual

132

a number of birds on the branches of the trees and on the lawn, and because they were tame, knowing that no Indian would hurt them, some were even sitting on the verandah-rail, hoping for crumbs from the break-fast-table.

"Yes, of course, the birds," Lord Branscombe said reflectively, as if he too noticed them for the first time.

He paused, then said slowly and, Latonia thought, deliberately:

"Perhaps they are hungry too."

As he spoke he took a *chipatti* from the basket, broke a small piece from it, and threw it towards the crows that were searching for worms amongst the sparse grass.

One, quicker than the rest, pounced on it and, taking it in his beak, flew off towards a tree.

He had practically reached the bough on which a number of other crows were sitting when his wings seemed to falter. . . .

A moment later he had fallen to the ground, a crumpled bunch of feathers, his head still moving for a second before it dropped forward and was still.

Latonia gave a little gasp but Lord Branscombe did not seem to notice, and, breaking off another piece of the *chipatti*, he threw it now high into the air.

A crow flew down, caught it in his beak, and flew straight upwards towards the roof from which he had come.

He flew only a little way from the verandah and even after his head had dropped his wings went on moving.

Lord Branscombe, without speaking, broke off another piece of the *chipatti*, but before he could throw it, his senior servant who had travelled with them came from the house to say:

"The carriage is waiting, Lord Sahib."

Lord Branscombe put the broken *chipatti* care-fully back into the basket on the table.

"In which case," he said to Latonia, "I think we should go now. We do not wish to keep the train waiting."

"No ... of course ... not," she answered.

Her voice sounded strange even to herself and she found it hard to take her eyes from the crows that were now motionless black spots on the green of the lawn.

A servant handed her her sunshade, her bag, and her gloves, and as they stepped into the carriage that was waiting outside, she saw that her small leather dressing-case was on the seat opposite them.

She knew that on Lord Branscombe's instructions their other luggage would be with their own servants in the carriage which followed behind.

There was no-one to bid them farewell and she was sure that Lord Branscombe was leaving earlier than he had previously announced.

He passed the Palace without even glancing in its direction, and now as they drove through the City Latonia felt fear rising within her like the movement of a snake.

The Rajah would have been told that Lord Branscombe had left and why, and this, she knew perceptively, was his real moment of danger as they drove first through the bazaar, the way they had come.

For the first time the silk-shops with their bales piled high in the shadows were not beautiful but threatening, and the stalls with their fruits, vegetables, and grain were not colourful but ominous.

Even the Brahmin bulls, taking their toll of the baskets of the vegetable-sellers, seemed more frightening than lazy.

As they passed, any hand that was raised seemed to Latonia to hold a dagger and every sound was the crack of a bullet.

For the first time since she had come to India she was not loving its people but hating them, and the children who she thought had smiled at her were now monsters jeering at her helplessness.

Because she was so afraid, she clenched her hands together to prevent herself from crying her fear aloud.

As they passed out into the open country, she looked at the bare rocks where a man with a rifle could hide and at the trees, wondering if there was an assailant concealed amongst their leaves.

One shot from any man who was skilled with a gun could kill Lord Branscombe so easily as they drove on in the open carriage, the horses moving rhythmically without hurry, their bridles jingling musically, while the sun turned everything to burnished gold.

In the distance ahead Latonia could see the railway-station and she knew that these were the last few moments the Rajah had in which to dispose of Lord Branscombe.

Once they reached the train they would be safe, and she wanted to ask him to crouch down on the floor of the carriage so that he would no longer be a target for those who wished to murder him.

But she knew that whatever plea she used, he would refuse her and undoubtedly would only despise her more than he did already, for such cowardice.

Because she felt so afraid as she waited tensely for the sound of a rifle being fired, she found it impossible to breathe and she shut her eyes.

She could only hold her breath and listen and wait, feeling as if her whole body had been turned to stone.

"Please ... God ... please ..."

Her prayers were still turning a little wheel round and round.

"Please ... please ..."

Then she felt the horses stop and opened her eyes.

They had reached the station.

For a moment she could not believe the journey was over, and yet now, because her feelings had been so intense, she could not move.

Somehow, with a superhuman effort, she stepped out of the carriage to cross the platform and climb into the train.

The train seemed like a sanctuary and as she turned to see that Lord Branscombe had followed her, she heard him say to the guard:

"We are ready to leave at once!"

The doors were shut and the whistle was blown, and as the wheels began to turn Latonia felt that her legs could no longer support her.

She put out her hand to save herself from falling, then as she did so, everything began to go dark. . . .

Someone was holding her, lifting her, and as she realised whose arms they were, she thought vaguely far away in the distance someone was saying:

"He is safe! He is safe!"

The next moment she felt herself laid down on the bed in her sleeping-compartment, but it was impossible to open her eyes. She felt Lord Branscombe take off her hat, then her shoes.

It seemed strange that he should concern himself with her, but her brain had ceased to function and she could only remember that he was safe and they had reached the station without his being murdered.

Then she heard him say:

"You must be very tired, Latonia, so I suggest you make up for last night by sleeping. We have a long journey in front of us and there is nothing to worry you now."

She tried to open her eyes and look at him, but it was impossible, so she turned her head sideways against the pillow like a child who wants to be comforted after being afraid.

She heard him go out quietly and close the door behind him.

*   *   *

Later, when Latonia had slept in what was the unconsciousness of exhaustion, she awoke to find that it was midday.

Remembering that Lord Branscombe had said they had a long journey in front of them, she undressed and got into bed and was nearly asleep when a steward brought her some food.

It was the usual Indian dish they had eaten so often before, of steaming rice and fiery hot vegetable-curry and with it several freshly baked *chipattis*.

She ate the curry but felt she could never look at a *chipatti* again without seeing the crows struggling against death as they writhed on the ground.

After she had eaten she felt a little stronger but at the same time still very tired, and she fell asleep thinking that the wheels beneath her were saying the same thing over and over again:

"He is safe! He is safe!"

* * *

Several hours later a Steward knocked on the door and told her that in half-an-hour they would be arriving and she should dress for riding.

He was gone before Latonia could formulate the question she had wanted to ask, which was, where were they going?

Then she told herself that it did not matter where it was. At least they were far away from the Rajah who wished to murder Lord Branscombe, and perhaps their next host would be more friendly and certainly less frightening.

She put on her riding-habit, not worrying particularly about her appearance because now that she felt rested she wanted only to see Lord Branscombe again and to ask him a thousand questions.

Although she hoped there would be time to talk before the train reached the station where they were to disembark, there were actually only a few minutes left when she went from her own compartment into the Drawing-Room.

Lord Branscombe was waiting and she saw that he had changed from his uniform into ordinary riding-clothes—white breeches and a thin, well-cut tussore jacket.

He looked exceedingly handsome, but what he was wearing made her aware that they were not to arrive with any pomp and she wondered why this particular Province would be different from the others they had visited.

For a moment she could only look at him, her eyes very large in her face, and think how wonderful it was that he was alive and not lying dead like the crows.

Then as his eyes met hers she felt as if her heart turned a somersault in her breast and she wanted to run to him and touch him to make sure that he was real and there was no longer any danger.

Instead she could only look away from him, her eye-lashes very dark against her pale cheeks.

As the train came to a shuddering standstill she held on to one of the chairs for support.

"I hope you are not too tired to ride."

"No ... of course not," Latonia replied. "I have been sleeping all day ... and I feel rather ashamed of my ... indolence."

"You have every excuse to be tired," Lord Branscombe replied. "I think neither of us found it easy to sleep last night."

There was no time for Latonia to answer.

The carriage door was opened, the servants were waiting, and she saw that they had stopped at a very small station, smaller even than the one at which they had alighted when they stopped the train to be married.

Latonia stepped down onto the platform wonderingly, then she looked up and drew in her breath.

High above them, peaking against the sky, were the snow-capped mountains of the Himalayas!

It was what she had always wanted to see, and

138

now that she saw them they were so exactly like her dreams that she thought she must still be asleep.

They seemed to blaze before her astonished eyes as if they were made of silver. Then before she could even take in what she was seeing, before she could speak the words of wonder which came to her lips, she found herself outside the station.

There were two horses waiting for her and Lord Branscombe and the usual caravan of other animals and servants to carry their luggage.

He helped her onto the saddle and they rode off. She found herself not wondering where they were going, but utterly and completely content to be beside him in the foothills of the Himalayas, where she had always wished to be.

After a few minutes they were away from the small village and now there were flowers such as Latonia had thought existed ony in Paradise; crimson, white, yellow, even blue.

They were magical in themselves, but it was impossible not to find her eyes being drawn upwards to where the mountains, silver with their gleaming peaks, were more lovely than it was possible to put into words.

They rode for a long time in silence, climbing all the time a road which at first had been wide enough for them to ride side-by-side but which now became a single track, and Lord Branscombe went ahead as if to lead the way while Latonia followed.

The sun was still very hot but she knew that when dusk fell the cold from the snows would be sharp and invigorating, and she could almost feel it now sweeping away her fatigue and everything except for a strange excitement which seemed to be rising within her.

"It is because I am seeing the Himalayas," she told herself.

But she knew, if she was truthful, that it was because she was with Lord Branscombe and she had the feeling that they were going somewhere where they might be alone and where he had no official business.

Still they went on climbing, and now the silver of the mountains had changed to gold and rose and she knew that soon the sun would be sinking.

Then suddenly ahead she saw a bungalow, white and newly painted, gleaming against the mountain-side almost as vividly as the snows high above it.

The flowers all round it were even more beautiful than those they had passed on their ride upwards, and as they drew nearer Latonia saw two Himalayan pheasants, the most spectacular birds in the world, scuttle away into the bushes.

They reached the bungalow and three servants came hurrying out to greet them.

There were two men and a middle-aged woman wearing a crimson sari, and they were bowing, smiling, and salaaming towards Lord Branscombe.

Then servants appeared and took their horses and they walked up some steps into one of the most attractive rooms which Latonia had ever seen.

The walls were white, with native woven rugs in brilliant colours on the floor.

There were flowers on the tables and there were chairs which were large and low and which obviously, she thought, had been designed for comfort.

Lord Branscombe was talking to the servants in their own language, and then, as Latonia stood looking round her, he said:

"It is getting late, and I expect you would like a bath. As soon as you are ready we will have dinner, for I know you have eaten little all day."

He was thinking of her, and she felt a warm glow sweep over her because he was speaking as if he really cared about how she was feeling.

"That would be lovely!" she replied. "But please tell me . . . to whom does this lovely house belong?"

"It belongs to me!" Lord Branscombe answered.

"I have owned it for some years and I always come here whenever I have a holiday."

"It is very beautiful!" Latonia said, but now she was looking through the window at the mountains, which were no longer gold- and rose-coloured but had turned to lilac and lavender in the dusk.

"I will tell you all about it later," Lord Branscombe said with a smile.

Because she knew it was what he wanted her to do, she followed him as he led her from the Sitting-Room into a bedroom which seemed surprisingly large for such a small bungalow.

There was a bed which looked like a galleon at sea, with a mosquito-net, which was quite unnecessary at this time of the year, draped like sails over the top of it, and there were curtains at the windows which were the blue of the sky when she had first seen the mountains silhouetted against it.

Surprisingly, there was a fireplace in which a fire had just been lit.

The woman in the red sari was waiting to attend to her and Latonia saw that some of her luggage had already been brought into the room.

"Your bath is ready, Lady Sahib," the woman said.

When Latonia answered her in Urdu, she smiled delightedly and chattered away quickly, and Latonia found it difficult to follow all she said but managed to understand the gist of it.

The bath, which was scented with a fragrance which Latonia knew could only have come from the flowers which grew in such profusion round the bungalow, swept away the last of her fatigue.

Now the excitement she had been feeling ever since she awoke seemed to grow and intensify until it vibrated within her like music.

By the time she had finished her bath, she found that the rest of her luggage had been brought to her room and the woman was unpacking it, filling a cupboard in the wall which stood open, and Latonia could see some of the pretty gowns which Toni had given her.

As Latonia began to dress she was drawn irresistibly to the window which looked out on the mountains.

Now they were in darkness except that the stars were coming out in the sky, and she thought that later there would be a moon.

She turned back to find that the woman had taken from the cupboard a very elaborate gown which Latonia, when she had found it amongst her things, had not expected she would ever be able to wear.

It was really a ball-gown, and with Lord Branscombe punishing her on board by keeping her in her cabin and telling her there would be no social engagements for her in India, she had thought it would be a gown that would remain unused on its hanger.

Now it struck her that it was very suitable for a bride, and although she dared not formulate it to herself, the obvious question seemed to be whether her husband would think of her as one.

She did not protest when the Indian woman helped her into it.

She had the feeling that it had been chosen not because it was white, which in India is worn only by widows, but because the tulle which decorated the hem and the decolletage sparkled with little drops of diamante like tiny stars.

Latonia felt they would echo the stars that were coming out in the sky, and there was a shining belt to encircle her small waist.

When she looked at herself in the mirror after she was dressed, she thought that in reality she should be wearing a tiara on her head and a necklace of diamonds at her throat.

As if the woman knew what she was thinking, she said in Urdu: "One moment, Lady Sahib!" and went from the room.

Sitting in front of the mirror, Latonia wondered where she had gone, but a few moments later she returned carrying in her hand some small buds of scented petals which Indian women wear at the backs of their heads.

Latonia had always admired them and thought they made all the women look attractive and very feminine.

Arranged skilfully in her own hair, they gave her a finish and what she felt was an attraction which she had never had before.

"Thank you, thank you!" she said.

The Indian woman smiled, saying:

"Lady Sahib very beautiful and Lord Sahib very handsome. Both blessed by god Krishna."

"I hope so," Latonia murmured beneath her breath.

Then, feeling very shy, she went from the bedroom into the Sitting-Room.

As she expected, Lord Branscombe was waiting for her.

He was wearing the evening-dress of the Bengal Lancers, and in some way he reminded her of the beautiful Himalayan pheasants she had seen hurrying away as they approached.

She walked towards him, meaning to say something light and amusing to relieve what she felt might be an awkward moment.

Then her eyes met his and it was impossible to speak, and, as if he felt the same, neither of them moved but just stood looking at each other.

A voice from the door made them start.

"Dinner is served, Lord Sahib!" a man-servant said, and they both looked as if it was an effort to remember what they must do.

Lord Branscombe offered Latonia his arm.

They walked into a small, attractive Dining-Room which was decorated with Rajput paintings which Latonia felt were not only beautiful but very valuable.

But for the moment she could not look at or think of anything except Lord Branscombe, and as they seated themselves at the table she saw that it was decorated with white flowers and she knew she had been right in wearing the gown which complemented them.

Later, it was difficult to remember what they had eaten, except that it had been delicious.

After the food on the train, which was always exactly the same, she thought the trout must have come from a mountain-stream and the rest of the dishes were all food that could be obtained locally and was fresh.

There was mango-juice to drink first, which Latonia thought was more delicious even than the wine which followed it, and which surprisingly was champagne.

Then as Lord Branscombe raised his glass she knew it was the inevitable drink for occasions such as they were celebrating, and she felt herself blush as he said:

"I want to treat this as our wedding-day and forget last night."

He paused before he added:

"Shall we drink to happiness? I think it is something we both want."

Latonia picked up her glass.

Because her heart was thumping so violently she felt it would be impossible for her to reply, but somehow in a voice little above a whisper she managed to say:

"I . . . I hope I may make you . . . happy."

"That is really what I should say to you," he answered, "but as we feel the same, shall we drink to it together?"

"Y-yes . . . of course," Latonia answered.

He touched her glass with his; then, as they both sipped their champagne, Latonia felt her breath coming quickly and once again it was impossible to meet Lord Branscombe's eyes.

When dinner was finished she rose to go back into the Sitting-Room and he followed her.

As if somehow someone had anticipated it was what she wished, the curtains were only partly drawn over the window which seemed to fill the whole of one wall, and now she looked out at the beauty before her, which for the moment swept everything else from her mind, even Lord Branscombe himself.

The moon had risen and everything was enveloped with a light that seemed to come from the gods themselves; the stars glittered in the darkness of the sky, and the peaks of the mountains glowed with brightness that made them seem almost as if they were alive and were in fact part of the Divine.

"It is so . . . lovely!" Latonia murmured.

"And so are you!" Lord Branscombe replied softly.

She was so surprised by his answer that she turned her face to look up at him.

As she did so she felt his arm go round her, and he said:

"This is where I thought you would want to spend your honeymoon."

"M-my . . . honeymoon?" Latonia faltered, feeling it was a word she had never expected to hear him say.

"The honeymoon that would never have happened," he said, "if you had not warned me as you did last night. It was very brave and very clever of you, and all today I have been thinking how lucky it was that you are with me."

"Do . . . do you . . . really mean that?" Latonia questioned.

She was feeling strange sensations pulsating through her because Lord Branscombe's arm was round her and he was close to her.

Then she said:

"Are you . . . safe . . . really safe now that we are here? You do not . . . think they will . . . follow you?"

Her voice for a moment held a frantic note. Then

she felt Lord Branscombe's arm tighten before he said:

"When you speak to me like that you make me feel as if you really care what happens to me."

"But of course I do!" Latonia said quickly, without thinking. "I have never been through such ... agony as today when I thought on the way to the station they would ... shoot you."

"I thought perhaps you were feeling like that," he said. "Was that why you nearly fainted when we reached the train?"

"Of course it was," Latonia replied, "but now you are safe! Please ... you must be careful ... very ... very careful in the future ... because ... I ..."

She was about to say:

"I could not bear to lose you," then thought it might be too revealing.

Her voice died away and after a moment Lord Branscombe said very softly:

"Will you finish that sentence?"

She shook her head. Then he said:

"I thought you hated me because I was punishing you, thinking you were Toni. You certainly appeared to dislike me until last night when I kissed you, and then I had an entirely different impression."

He felt Latonia tremble in his arms and saw the blush rise in her cheeks.

She made as if to hide it from him, and after a moment he said very gently:

"When I kissed you, Latonia, I thought no woman's lips could be so soft, so sweet, unless she felt what I felt."

Latonia stiffened, then she said in a voice he could barely hear:

"What ... did you ... feel?"

"What I have been feeling for a long time," Lord Branscombe answered, "and although I fought against it and was horrified at the idea of it, I found it inescapable. Then last night I admitted it was— love."

His voice deepened on the word and Latonia asked:

"Are you . . . saying that you . . . love me . . . a little?"

"I love you as I have never loved anyone before," Lord Branscombe replied. "Do you not understand the agonies you have made me suffer?"

She looked up at him enquiringly, and he said with a somewhat wry smile on his lips:

"I thought you were my niece. I was horrified at the feelings I had for you, and shocked."

Latonia drew a deep breath.

"You . . . loved . . . me?"

"I fell in love with you when I was teaching you Urdu and found how quick-brained and intelligent you were. Your mind excited and inspired me every time you talked to me."

"I thought you . . . despised me."

"I tried to feel for you what I felt for Toni when I heard of the way she had behaved with young Luddington and other men—but I failed!"

"I am . . . glad," Latonia said. "I wanted so . . . much that you should . . . admire me and . . . like me."

"How could I know that?" Lord Branscombe asked. "All I could think was that because of my feelings, I must send you out of my life, and yet every instinct in my body wanted you to stay. Oh, my darling, how could you have done this to me?"

The way he spoke and the endearment made Latonia turn her face to hide it against his shoulder.

His arms still held her very close and she felt his lips on her hair before he said:

"Long before last night I knew I loved you, and when you came to me so bravely to save my life and behaved with courage and intelligence such as only one woman in a million would have shown, I knew I had found the perfect wife I have always been seeking."

"Y-you really . . . mean that?"

"Let me convince you."

As Lord Branscombe spoke, he put his fingers under her chin and turned her face up to his.

For a moment he looked down at her as if he must impress her beauty on his mind for all time, then his lips were on hers.

As he kissed her Latonia knew that this was what she had been wanting and longing for.

Now his kiss was even more wonderful than it had been the night before, and she felt that the flowers and the mountains, the moonlight and the stars, even the gods themselves came down from their hiding-places and made both her and Lord Branscombe part of themselves.

He kissed her until she was no longer herself but his.

Then there was nothing else, not even the moon and the stars, but only his arms and his lips. . . .

* * *

A long time later Latonia whispered against Lord Branscombe's shoulder:

"I . . . love . . . you!"

He held her a little closer, and in the firelight which cast a golden light over the room Latonia could see his eyes looking at her with an expression of so much love that she wanted to cry out at the wonder of it.

He swept her hair back from her forehead with his free hand before he said:

"How can you be so perfect? I keep trying to find a flaw in your perfection, but it is impossible, and now I know I am the most fortunate man in the whole world because you belong to me."

"It is . . . true . . . it is . . . really true?" Latonia asked. "I am your . . . wife . . . but . . . I shall always be afraid of . . . losing you."

"Because I would not have you worried," Lord Branscombe replied, "I will not undertake any more investigations like the one I have just done."

"You . . . promise me that?"

"It is an easy thing to promise," he answered, "because I happen to know that the Viceroy has a very different task for me in the future."

"What is that?" Latonia asked apprehensively.

"I am to be made a Governor," Lord Branscombe explained, "and I know that no Governor will have a wife who is more suitable and more helpful to him than you will be to me, my darling."

"Is that true ... really true?"

"When our honeymoon is over we will go down to Calcutta and you will know then that what I am telling you is the truth."

"I am glad ... very glad. I love you so desperately! I do not think I could bear again to go through the agonies I went through today."

"Now you know what I have been feeling for weeks."

He pulled her a little closer to him before he said in a voice which she found hard to recognise:

"If I had been obliged to lose you, then I think I would have welcomed the 'apple of death' rather than go on living alone."

"You must not say such things!" Latonia cried. "You are so wonderful, so magnificent in every way, that whether I was in your life or not, there would always be work for you to do, and I am quite certain India could not do without you."

"I am not concerned with India at the moment," he answered, "but with you, and I know, my precious, that neither of us can do without the other. How, here in the shadow of the Himalayas, could we not be aware that this is not the first time we have met and our love is ageless?"

"That is what ... I feel too. Papa used to talk to me about reincarnation, and I always prayed that I would meet someone whom I had loved before and who had loved me."

She gave a little sigh of exasperation as she said:

"I am so angry with myself that I did not feel that you were that person from the moment I saw you."

"I ought to have felt the same," Lord Branscombe admitted, "but it was not long, my sweet, before I felt the magnetism about you holding me compellingly captive, however hard I fought against it."

"I am so . . . glad you felt like . . . that."

"I had intended to make you marry Andrew Luddington."

Latonia gave a cry of horror.

"How could you? How could you think of anything so wrong and wicked?"

"I wanted to be free of a love that was growing day by day, and because I knew it was wrong, I thought that the only way would be for you to be married to somebody else."

"How could you think I would do . . . anything so . . . horrible?"

Lord Branscombe smiled.

"I have a feeling you would have refused to do so, but the situation never really arose. So now we can forget all that unhappiness and remember only that we are together as fate meant us to be."

"It is . . . our Karma," Latonia whispered.

"A very wonderful, very perfect Karma as far as I am concerned," Lord Branscombe said, "and which will grow more perfect year by year."

"I . . . want to make you . . . happy."

"I am happier now than I have ever been in my whole life," he replied, "because you are mine, my precious little love, and I shall look after you, protect you, and never again will I allow you to deceive me."

"And you forgive me for doing so?"

"Not completely. I intend to go on punishing you—but with—kisses."

Latonia moved a little closer.

"I would . . . like that. . . ."

He kissed her and felt her body quiver against his.

"I love you!" he exclaimed. "God, how I love you!"

His fingers encircled the softness of her neck.

"If you ever stop loving me," he said fiercely, "I think I would kill you."

"I love you ... I love you with my heart, my mind, and ... my soul. They are all yours."

She felt his hand moving lower, touching her breast as he said very softly:

"And your body?"

"That is ... yours too. Please ... believe me."

"I believe you," he answered. "But, my beautiful darling, you must prove your love again and again."

As he spoke his lips were on hers, and as he kissed her Latonia felt as if the flames from the fire were flickering within her and growing more insistent until they touched her lips and met the flames that burnt in Lord Branscombe.

Then she knew that there was no need to prove their love with words, for the gods came down once again to envelop them with their Divine light and they were one, in a love which came from eternity and would continue into eternity.

The love which never dies.

ABOUT THE AUTHOR

BARBARA CARTLAND, the world's most famous romantic novelist, who is also an historian, playwright, lecturer, political speaker and television personality, has now written over 200 books.

She has also had many historical works published and has written four autobiographies as well as the biographies of her mother and that of her brother Ronald Cartland, who was the first Member of Parliament to be killed in the last war. This book has a preface by Sir Winston Churchill.

Barbara Cartland has sold 100 million books over the world, more than half of these in the U.S.A. She broke the world record in 1975 by writing twenty books, and her own record in 1976 with twenty-one. In addition, her album of love songs has just been published, sung with the Royal Philharmonic Orchestra.

In private life, Barbara Cartland, who is a Dame of the Order of St. John of Jerusalem, has fought for better conditions and salaries for Midwives and Nurses. As President of the Royal College of Midwives (Hertfordshire Branch), she has been invested with the first Badge of Office ever given in Great Britain which was subscribed to by the Midwives themselves. She has also championed the cause for old people and founded the first Romany Gypsy Camp in the world.

Barbara Cartland is deeply interested in Vitamin Therapy and is President of the British National Association for Health.